Among Malay Pirates

A Tale Of Adventure And Peril

And Other Tales Of Adventure And Peril

by

G. A. Henty

Loki's Publishing

Contents

CHAPTER I

"I wish most heartily that something would happen," Harry Parkhurst, a midshipman of some sixteen years of age, said to his chum, Dick Balderson, as they leaned on the rail of her majesty's gunboat Serpent, and looked gloomily at the turbid stream that rolled past the ship as she lay at anchor.

"One day is just like another—one is in a state of perspiration from morning till night, and from night till morning. There seems to be always a mist upon the water; and if it were not that we get up steam every three or four days and run out for twenty-four hours for a breath of fresh air, I believe that we should be all eaten up with fever in no time. Of course, they are always talking of Malay pirates up the river kicking up a row; but it never seems to come off."

"There is one thing, Harry—there is always something to look at, for there are canoes constantly going up and down, and there is plenty of variety among them—from the sluggish dhows, laden with up country produce, to the long canoes with a score of paddlers and some picturesque ruffian sitting in the stern. It adds to the interest when you know that the crews are cutthroats to a man, and would make but the shortest possible work of you if they had got you in their power."

"Yes, Dick. Look at that canoe coming up stream; what a good looking chap that is in the stern, though by the way he scowls at us I can quite believe he would, as you say, cut our throats if he had the chance. That is a pretty little child sitting by him, and what a gorgeous dress she has! There, you see, he can look pleasant enough when he speaks to her. I fancy they must have come from a long way up the river, for they look wilder than most of the fellows who pass us. If that fool who is steering her does not mind what he is about, Dick, he will either run into that canoe coming down or else get across our chain. There, I told you so."

The man at the tiller was in fact, looking, with mingled curiosity and hostility, at the gunboat that he was passing but a few yards away, and did not notice a canoe, manned by six rowers, that was coming down with the stream, taking an oblique course across the bows of the Serpent, and was indeed hidden from his view by the hull of the vessel, until he had passed beyond her. Then there was a sudden shout and a yell from a dozen throats, as the two canoes came into collision, the one proceeding up the river being struck on the quarter with a force that almost cut her in two, and in an instant her occupants were in the water. As the Malays were to a man almost as much at home in the water as on land, the accident would have had little effect beyond the loss of the boat and its contents, had it not been that the stern of the other craft struck the Malay chief with such force as to completely disable him, and he would have sunk at once had not two of the boatmen grasped him and kept his head above water.

"What has become of the child?" Harry Parkhurst exclaimed, and he and Dick Balderson both leaped on to the rail, throwing off their jackets as they shouted to the men to lower a boat. Nothing could be seen of the child until, after half a minute's suspense, a little face suddenly appeared in the swirl of the muddy water some fifteen yards from the vessel's side. It was gone again in an instant, but, as it disappeared, both lads sprang from the side and with a few strokes reached the spot where they had seen the face disappear; then they dived under water and soon grasped her. As soon as they came to the surface a sailor, who had seized a coil of rope, flung it to them, and, grasping it, they were quickly by the side of the gunboat.

A minute later some sailors, who had at once tumbled into a boat on the alarm being given, came up. The child was first handed into it, then the midshipmen scrambled in, and, by their directions, two of the sailors, standing on the thwarts, lifted the child high above their heads to the hands of the men leaning over the bulwark.

"Take the little thing to the doctor," Dick said. "Now, lads, row on; let's pick up some of those Malay fellows."

A babel of shouts and sounds rose from the water; the bow of the second canoe had been stove in, and she also had sunk to the water level; a fierce fight was going on between several of the Malays; the chief, who was being supported by two of his crew, was shouting furiously; and others of his men, in obedience to his orders, were diving under water. Harry turned to the gunboat, and called to the men to bring Soh Hay, the interpreter, to the side. A minute later the man was hustled to the rail.

"Tell that chief that we have got his child safely on board," Harry shouted.

Again and again the interpreter called out; but it was some time before he could make the chief pay attention to him. As the latter caught the purport of his words his face changed at once, and, after calling to his men to desist from their search, his head sank on to the shoulder of one of the men supporting him, and he evidently lost consciousness.

"He is badly hurt, Dick; we had better get him on board, too. Old Horsley was wishing this morning that he had something to do beyond administering doses of quinine to the men."

Taking the tiller, he brought the boat alongside the chief, and four of the sailors, directed by Dick, gently raised him from the water and laid him on the bottom of the boat. Blood was flowing freely from an ugly gash in his face, and it was evident from the manner in which his left arm hung limp, as they lifted him up, that either the shoulder or the arm itself was broken.

"Get him alongside at once, lads," Dick said. "I expect he is more injured than we see. The other fellows will be all right; they can all swim like fish."

In two or three minutes the injured man was laid down under an awning over the fore deck of the cruiser, and the surgeon at once came up.

"How is the child, Doctor?"

"She is still insensible," he said, "but she will soon be all right. I can't discover any injury, and I think it likely that it was the sudden shock, and perhaps a knock against the side of the boat, that stunned her; for I have no doubt she could swim, small as she is. This is a much more serious affair; he has an ugly gash in his temple, his collarbone is broken, and," he went on, as he passed his hands down the patient's side, "he has two, if not more ribs broken."

"Well, we will leave him to you, Doctor; there are a lot of these fellows in the water, and I suppose they must be brought on board until we can get a boat to take them ashore."

In a few minutes eighteen Malays were brought to the side, and the two canoes, which were floating level with the water, were towed up and fastened by a rope to the stern of the gunboat. Even when safely on deck, the two parties were still so infuriated that they had to be separated and placed under guards apart from each other. Three or four had been killed by the stabs of the deadly krises, and their bodies could be seen floating astern. Several of those rescued had wounds more or less severe.

"We should not have much chance with those fellows in the water, Mr. Parkhurst," an old sailor said to Harry.

"No, indeed, Davis; they could swim round and round us, and our cutlasses would be very little good against those ugly looking krises. If we were to leave them to themselves, they would fight to the death; and, after all, it was no one's fault in particular. Mr. Balderson and I were watching them; one was crossing the ship's bow just as the other came out from her side, and they were into each other before either had time to hold their boat up."

"That chap the doctor is bandaging up was in a nice taking about his child, sir; it was a lucky job that you and Mr. Balderson happened to catch sight of her."

"Yes, poor little thing! It was only just a glimpse we got of her face; but as we were looking for her, and ready to dive, it was enough."

"Lucky we are inside the bar, Mr. Parkhurst, or the sharks would have had half the fellows."

"I did not think of it at the time, Davis, and it would not have made any difference if I had; we were only in the water a couple of minutes, and the Malays were making noise enough to frighten away any number of sharks. You will have the job of washing out our trousers again—we had only put them on clean half an hour before."

"That aint no matter, sir, especially if you go down and change at once; the mud will come out easy enough if I leave them in a bucket of fresh water for half an hour."

The two midshipmen joined the group of officers who were standing near the doctor; the latter had, on closer examination, announced that four of the ribs were broken. He had finished his work just as the lads came up. News had been brought up by the steward that the little girl had opened her eyes; while he was speaking, the Malay conversed rapidly with the interpreter.

"What is he saying, Soh Hay?" the captain asked.

"He is asking why his daughter is not here, and if she is hurt, and how she came to be saved," the man replied. "Me tell him she come up to see him soon; the doctor say she no hurt."

Two minutes later the doctor reappeared, carrying the child in his arms. She looked round fearlessly at the white faces until her eye fell upon her father, when she slipped out of the doctor's arms like an eel and ran to him. The grim features of the Malay lit up with a pleasant smile as he held out his right hand to her. She was a strange little figure, for the doctor had not waited to obtain any suitable garments for her, but had wrapped her up in one of the signal flags, which the child herself had wound round her waist and over her shoulder like a native sarong.

"You tell him, Soh Hay, that he must not talk to her," the doctor said. "If he keeps quiet, he will get well in short time: if he talk, he ill many days; but I will let him say a few words to her now."

The Malay's eyes passed over the group of officers and rested on the two midshipmen, whose wet clothes showed that they were the officers who had, as the interpreter had told him, dived in and rescued the child. He said something to the interpreter.

"Malay man want to speak to you, young gentlemen," the man said; "he wish to thank you."

"Oh, tell him there is nothing to thank us for," Harry said hastily; "it was nothing more than taking a bath."

"Yes, officer, but he wishes to speak to you."

Somewhat reluctantly, the two lads approached the side of the injured man; he took each of them by the hand, and, as he did so, said something which Soh Hay interpreted:

"The chief says that you have given him back what he loved best in the world, and that his life is yours whenever it may be of use to you; he may be of service to you, gentlemen, should you ever go up the river—a Malay never forgives an injury or forgets a service."

"Tell him we are very glad to have brought his little girl out of the water," Harry said, "and that if we ever go up the river, we will pay him a visit."

The chief was now laid in a cot which was swung from the stanchions of the awning, while the little girl was carried away by the doctor, who laid her in a berth, gave her a cup of tea, which she drank obediently to his orders, but evidently regarded as being extremely nasty, and she was then told through the interpreter to go to sleep until her sarong was dried. A couple of hours later she was on deck again in her native garb and ornaments. The interpreter pointed out to her the two midshipmen who had rescued her, and she at once went up to them, and, slipping her hands into theirs, began to prattle freely; they were unable to understand what she said, but they took her round the ship, showing her the guns, and introduced her to Ponto, the captain's great Newfoundland, who submitted gravely to be patted by her; to Jacko, the monkey, who was by no means disposed to be friendly, but chattered and showed his teeth; and to Julius Caesar, the negro cook, who grinned from ear to ear, and presented her with some cakes from a batch which he had just made for the captain's table.

The rest of the Malays had already left the ship; two native boats had been hailed, and in these the two parties of Malays had taken their places, and, with their boats towing behind, had been rowed away, the captain giving strict instructions that they were to be landed on opposite sides of the river. The little maid speedily became a general pet on board the Serpent, and was soon the proud possessor of several models of ships, two patchwork quilts, several carved tobacco boxes, and other specimens of sailors' handiwork. Small as she was, she had evidently a strong idea of her own importance, and received these presents and attentions with a pretty air of dignity which at once earned for her the title of the Princess.

On the second day after the accident, the chief's boat came off from the shore, the damage having been speedily and neatly repaired. Little Bahi stood on the top of the accommodation ladder as they approached, and addressed them with great asperity, using much gesticulation with her arms.

"What is she saying, Soh Hay?" Dick Balderson asked.

"She is telling them that they are bad men to let the boat be run down; that she is very angry with them, and they will all be punished."

'The men looked very crestfallen under their little mistress' reproaches, and held up their hands in a deprecating manner; while the helmsman stood up and, after salaaming deeply, entered upon a long explanation, which ended in his asking if he might come on board to see his chief. Permission was at once granted by the captain, upon the request being interpreted to him. When he mounted the steps, Bahi led him to the side of her father's cot. The doctor, however, interposed.

"Tell him he must not talk," he said to the interpreter; "the chief is ill and must not be allowed to excite himself. But he can say a few words, if he wants to."

The cot had been lowered to within a few inches of the deck in order that the chief might watch his daughter as she trotted about and romped with Ponto, who had now quite taken her into his friendship. The chief's face expressed alarm when he first saw the great dog; but when he saw how gentle the animal was, and how, when one of the sailors placed the child on his back, it walked gravely up and down the deck, wagging its tail as if pleased with its novel burden, he was satisfied that no harm could come to her from this formidable looking animal. He had first spoken a few words sharply to the man in answer to his excuses, and, indeed, had the helmsman been minding his business instead of looking at the ship, the collision might have been prevented; but Hassan Jebash was at the present moment so well contented with the recovery of his child that he accepted the man's excuses, and the latter went back to his boat evidently greatly relieved.

In a few days the chief began to show signs of impatience, and through the interpreter constantly demanded of the doctor when he would be well enough to leave.

"You ask him, Soh Hay, whether he wishes to be able to lead his tribe in battle again, or to go through life unable to use a kris or hurl a spear. In another ten days, if he remains quiet, he will be able to go, and in a couple of months will be as strong and active as ever, if he will but keep quiet until the bones have knit. Surely a chief is not like an impatient child, ready to risk everything for the sake of avoiding a little trouble."

The chief, on this being translated to him, scowled angrily.

"Tell him it is of no use his scowling at me, Soh Hay. I am not doctoring him for my own amusement, but for his good, and because he is the father of that little child."

The chief, when this was translated to him, lay without speaking for two or three minutes, and then said quietly, "Tell the doctor I am sorry; he is right, and I have been foolish. I will stay till he says I may go."

CHAPTER II

Four or five days later the chief was allowed to get up and to walk quietly up and down the deck, and a week afterwards the doctor said, "You can go now, chief, if you desire it; but you must be content to keep quiet for another couple of months, and not make any great exertions or move quickly. How long will it take you to go up the river to your home?"

"Six days' easy paddling."

"Well, that is in your favor; but do not travel fast. Take it quietly, and be as long as you can on the voyage—lying in a canoe is as good a rest as you can take."

"Thank you, Doctor, I will obey your instructions. You have all been very kind to me, and a Malay chief never forgets benefits. I have been hostile to the white men, but now I see I have been mistaken, and that you are good and kind. Is it true that your boat is going up the river? Soh Hay tells me that it is so."

"Yes; one of the chiefs, Sehi Pandash, wishes to place himself under our protection, and he has sent to ask that the ship might go up and fire her big guns, that the tribes round may see that he has strong friends who can help him."

"It is two days' rowing up the river to my place from his, and when you are there I shall come down to see you. Sehi is not a good chief; he quarrels with his neighbors, and shelters their slaves who run away to him; he is not a good man."

"Well, we shall all be glad to see you, chief, and I hope that you will bring your daughter with you. She has won all our hearts, and we shall miss her sadly."

"I will bring her if I can do so safely," the chief said gravely; "but I am no friends with Sehi; he stops my trade as it comes down the river, and takes payment for all goods that pass down. It is because he knows that many of us are angered that he wishes to put himself under your protection. I think that you do not do well to aid so bad a fellow."

"We did not know that he was a bad fellow, chief. The best plan will be for you and the other chiefs who are aggrieved to send down complaints against him, or to come down yourselves when we are up there and talk it over with our Captain, who will doubtless impress upon Sehi the necessity for abstaining from such practices, and that he cannot expect aid from us if he embroils himself with his neighbors by interfering with their trade. Is he strong?"

"He has many war prahus, which sometimes come down to the sea and return with plunder, either collected from the cultivators near the coast or from trading ships captured and burnt."

"I will mention what you tell me to the Captain, and it will prepare him to listen to any complaint that may be made to him. But you must remember that he is only acting under the orders of the Governor of the Straits Settlements, and must refer all important matters to him."

"I will come when you are there," Hassan said gravely. "If nothing is done, there will be war."

There was general regret on board the Serpent when the little princess said goodby to all her friends and went down the accommodation ladder to the boat with her father. The chief had said but little to the two young midshipmen, for he saw that they preferred that the matter should not be alluded to, but he held their hands at parting, and said:

"I shall see you again before long; but if at any time you should want me, I will come, even if your summons reach me in the middle of a battle."

"It is such nonsense, Doctor," Harry said, as the boat pushed off, "to have so much made of such a thing as jumping into the water. If one had been alone, and had tried to save a man or a woman, in such a state of funk that there was a good chance of their throwing their arms round your neck and pulling you down with them, there might be something in it, though everyone takes his chance of that when he jumps in to save anyone from drowning; but with a little child, and two of us to do it, and the ship close at hand, it was not worth thinking of for a moment."

"No, Parkhurst, from your point of view the thing was not, as you say, worth giving a thought to; but, you see, that is not the point of view of the chief. To him it is nothing whether your exploit was a gallant one or not, or whether you ran any danger; the point simply is, his child would have been drowned had you not seen her and fished her out, and that it is to you that he owes her life. I think you have reason to congratulate yourselves on having made a friend who may be very useful to you. It may be that there will be trouble up the river; and if so, he might possibly be of real service to you. But in any case he may be able to give you some good hunting and fishing, and show you things that you would never have had an opportunity of seeing without his friendship and assistance."

"I did not think of that, Doctor; yes, that would certainly be a great thing."

"I can assure you I look at it in that light myself, Parkhurst, and I am looking forward to paying him a visit, as, under his protection, I should get opportunities of collecting which I could never have in the ordinary way; for, unless they are greatly maligned, one could not trust one's self among the Malays without some special protection."

"But they are not savages, Doctor. Hassan is a perfect gentleman in manner, and in that silk jacket of his and handsome sarong he really looks like a prince. I could not help thinking that all of us looked poor creatures by his side."

"They certainly cannot be called savages, though from our point of view many of their customs are of a very savage nature. Piracy is very general among those living on the seacoast or on the great rivers; but it must be remembered that it is not so very many centuries ago that a toll was demanded of all passersby by the barons having castles on the Rhine and other navigable rivers; the crews of wrecked ships were plundered on every coast of Europe, our own included, not so very long ago; and in the days of Elizabeth, Drake and Hawkins were regarded by the Spaniards as pirates of the worst class, and I fear that there was a good deal of justice in the accusation. But the Malays are people with a history; they believe themselves that they were the original inhabitants of the island of Sumatra; however, it is certain that in the twelfth century they had extended their rule over the whole of that island and many of its neighbors, and in the thirteenth had established themselves on this peninsula and had founded an empire extending over the greater part of the islands down to the coast of Australia. They had by this time acquired the civilization of India, and their sultans were powerful monarchs. They carried on a great trade with China, Hindoostan, and Siam, and their maritime code was regulated and confirmed, as early as 1276, by Mohammed Shah."

"How is it that they have come to such grief, Doctor?"

"Principally by the fact that they had the feudal, or you may call it the tribal, system. Each petty chief and his followers made war on his neighbors if he was strong enough; and as some tribes conquered others, the empire became split up into an indefinite number of clans, whose chiefs paid but a very nominal allegiance to the sultan. So islands broke off from the empire until it had practically ceased to exist, and the Malays were a people united only by similar customs and language, but in no other respect, and were, therefore, able to offer but slight resistance on the arrival of the Dutch and Portuguese in these regions. Still, the upper classes preserve the memory of their former greatness. The people are intelligent, and most of the trade in this part of the world is carried on by them. They are enterprising, and ready to emigrate if they see a chance of improving their fortunes. You know we saw many of them at the Cape when we touched there. Nominally they are Mohammedans in religion; but they do not strictly observe the ordinances of the Koran, and their Mohammedanism is mixed up with traces of their original religion."

"Ah, that explains why the chief's name was Hassan. I wondered that a Malay should have a Mohammedan name. They are not much like Arabs in figure. Of course, Hassan is a very fine looking man, and some of the other chiefs we saw at Penang were so; but most of them are shorter than we are, and very ugly."

"Yes, in figure and some other points they much resemble the Burmese, who are probably blood relations of theirs. The chiefs are finer men, as you will always find in the case in savage or semi savage peoples, for, of course, they have the pick of the women, and naturally choose the best looking. Their food, too, is better and their work less rough than that of the people at large.

"The sons and daughters of the chiefs naturally intermarry, and the result is that in most cases you will find the upper classes taller, better formed, lighter in color, and of greater intelligence than the rest of the people. This would be specially the case in a trading people like the Malays; their ships would bring over girls purchased in India, just as the ruling classes in Turkey used to obtain their wives from Circassia; and this, no doubt, has helped to modify the original Malay type."

"Thank you, Doctor; I think I shall like the Malays now I know something about them. Is it true that they are so treacherous?"

"I don't know, Parkhurst; doubtless they are treacherous in their wars; that is to say that they consider any means fair to deceive an enemy; but I do not think that they are so, beyond that. The Dutch have never had any very great difficulty with them, nor have we in the portion of the peninsula where we have established our rule. Of course, I know little about them myself, as I have only been out here a few months; but I am told that as traders they can be trusted, and that the word of a Malay chief can be taken with absolute confidence. Of course, among the majority of the people of the peninsula we are regarded with jealousy and hostility—they dread that we should extend our dominion over them, and it is not surprising that they should by every means in their power strive to prevent our coming far inland. The chiefs on the rivers are, as a rule, specially hostile.

"In the first place, because their towns and villages are more accessible to us, and they know more of our power than those dwelling in the hill country; and, secondly, because they depend largely upon the revenue that they derive from taxing all goods passing up and down, and which they not unreasonably think they might lose if we were to become paramount. No doubt there is much that Hassan said of Sehi that is true and is applicable to other chiefs who have placed themselves under our protection—namely, that they have so injured trade by their exactions as to incur the hostility of their neighbors. Of course, I am not speaking of such men as the Rajahs of Johore and Perac, who are enlightened men, and have seen the benefits to be derived from intercourse with us. Their people are agriculturists, and they are really on a par with the protected states in India.

"There is a great future before the country; gold is found in many of the rivers, tin is probably more abundant than in any other part of the world, and the exports are now very large; there are immense quantities of valuable timber, such as teak, sandalwood, and ebony. The climate is, except on the low land near the rivers, very healthy; nutmegs, cloves, and other spices can be grown there, and indigo, chocolate, pepper, opium, the sugarcane, coffee, and cotton, are all successfully cultivated. Some day, probably, the whole peninsula will fall under our protection, and when the constant tribal feuds are put a stop to, the forests cleared, and the ground cultivated, as is the case in our own settlement of Malacca, it will be found one of the most valuable of our possessions. Any amount of labor can be obtained from China, and it is probable that the races who inhabit the mountainous districts, who are said to be industrious and peaceable, will also readily adapt themselves to the changed conditions. They are not Malays like the people of the lowlands, but are a black race with curly wool, like the natives of Africa, and probably inhabited the whole peninsula before the arrival of the Malays."

"How funny that there should be niggers here," Harry said.

"They are not exactly negroes, but one of the races known as negritos, having, of course, many negro characteristics, but differing from the African negroes in some important particulars. To them our supremacy would be an unmixed blessing; their products would reach the coast untaxed, and they would obtain all European goods at vastly cheaper rates. A minor benefit to be obtained by our supremacy is that our sportsmen would certainly speedily diminish the number of wild beasts that at present are a scourge to cultivators; the tigers would be killed down, the elephants captured and utilized, and the poor people would not see their plantations ravaged, but would be able to travel through their forests without the constant danger of being carried off by tigers and panthers, and possibly be able to cross their rivers without the risk of being snapped up by alligators; though, doubtless, it would take some time before this would be brought about."

"And when do you think that we shall be going up the river, Doctor?"

"That I cannot say. The Captain has been expecting orders ever since we came here, six weeks ago; but possibly something may have been learned of Sehi's characteristics, and there may be doubts as to the expediency of taking under our protection a chief whose conduct appears to be anything but satisfactory. On the other hand, it may be considered that by so doing we may establish some sort of influence over the surrounding tribes, and so make a step towards promoting trade and putting a stop to these tribal wars, that are the curse of the country."

"It would be an awful sell if they were to change their minds," Harry exclaimed.

"I should be sorry myself, Parkhurst, for you know I am a collector. But I can tell you that you won't find it all sport and pleasure. You will have no cool sea breezes; there will be occasion for continual watchfulness, and perhaps long boat expeditions up sluggish streams, in an atmosphere laden with moisture and miasma."

"One expects some drawbacks, Doctor."

"You will find a good many, I can tell you, youngster. Still, I hope we shall go up; and I think that we shall do so, for it will be the Captain's report that will help the authorities to decide whether to appoint a Resident there or not."

A fortnight later a small dispatch boat steamed in and the news soon spread through the ship that the Serpent was to ascend the river on the following day. All was at once bustle and animation. Sailors like anything for a change, and all were impatient at the long delay that had occurred.

CHAPTER III

The gunboat was a large one, and carried two midshipmen besides Parkhurst and Balderson, who were, however, their seniors. The mess consisted of the four lads, a master's mate, the doctor's assistant, and the paymaster's clerk. In the gun room were the three lieutenants, the doctor, the lieutenant of the marines, and the chief engineer. The crew consisted of a hundred and fifty seamen and forty marines; the Serpent having a somewhat strong complement. She had been sent out specially for service in the rivers, being of lighter draught than usual, with unusually airy and spacious decks, and so was well fitted for the work. The conversation in the junior mess of the Serpent was very lively that evening. The vessel since her arrival on the station had made two runs between Singapore and Penang, but those on board had seen but little of the country, and were delighted at the thought of a possibility of active service, and the talk was all of boat expeditions, attacks from piratical prahus, of the merits of the bayonet and rifle opposed to kris and spear, and of sporting expeditions in which elephants, tigers, and other wild beasts were to fall victims of their prowess.

"You will find that you won't get much of that," the mate, who was president of the mess, said, after listening to their anticipations of sport. "I have been on the west coast of Africa and know what it is poking about in muddy creeks in boats, tramping through the jungle, knee deep in mud, half the crew down with fever, and the rest worn out with work and heat. I can tell you it is not all fun, as you youngsters seem to think, but downright hard work."

"Ah, well! any amount of work is better than standing here doing nothing," Dick said cheerfully, for the mate was known as a proverbial grumbler. He had been unfortunate, and, as is usually the case, his misfortunes were in some degree due to himself, for he was fond of liquor, and although, when on board, he took no more than his share, he was often somewhat unsteady in his speech when he returned from a run ashore; and although the matter was not grave enough for his captains to report altogether unfavorably of him, it was sufficiently so for them to shrink from recommending him for promotion, and in consequence he had seen scores of younger men raised over his head. He had been for some time unemployed before he had joined the Serpent, and had been appointed to her only because Captain Forest, who was a friend of his family, had used his interest on his behalf. He had, however, when he joined, spoken frankly to him.

"I have asked for you, Morrison," he said, "simply for the sake of your father; but I tell you frankly, that unless my report is a thoroughly favorable one, you are not likely to be again employed. I was told that there was nothing special against you, but that in no case since you passed have you been warmly spoken of. It has been said that you know your duty well; but they had privately learned that you were fond of liquor; and although no charge of absolute drunkenness had been brought against you, it was considered that you would not make a desirable officer in a higher rank. Now your future depends upon yourself; if you have the resolution to give up the habit, you may yet retrieve yourself. If I find that you do so, I shall certainly take the opportunity of giving you a chance to distinguish yourself, and shall strongly urge your claim to promotion. If I am not able to do this, you must make up your mind to be permanently put upon the shelf."

The admonition had not been in vain, and since joining the Serpent Morrison had made a successful effort to break himself of the habit. He had very seldom gone ashore, and when he did so, never went alone, and always returned at an early hour, and without having taken more than he would have done in the ordinary way on board. He had not, however, given up his habit of grumbling, and his messmates were so accustomed to his taking a somber view of everything that his prognostication as to the nature of their work up the river had but little effect upon them.

"What do you think, Sandy?" Harry Parkhurst asked the Scotch assistant surgeon.

"I know nothing about it, except what I have read. They say that the country is healthy; but it stands to reason that this cannot be so while you have got rivers with swamps and jungles and such heat as this. However, we have a good supply of quinine on board, and with that and our allowance of spirits, I hope that we shan't, as Morrison says, have half the ship's company down with the fever. It is all in our favor that we have only just come out, for they say that newcomers can resist the effects of these tropical rivers much better than those whose constitution has been weakened by a residence in the country. As to the sport, I have no desire to kill any animal that does not meddle with me. My business is all the other way, and if any of you get mauled, I will do my best to help the doctor to pull you through; but I am very well on board the ship, and have no desire to go tramping about among the swamps, whether it be to hunt animals or fight Malays."

"You think that everyone should stick to his last, Sandy," Dick said with a laugh. "Well, I only wish there were more on board of your opinion, for that would give more chances to us who like to stretch our legs ashore for a change."

"I can stretch my legs here if I want to," the Scotchman said quietly, "and am not anxious to do more. I suppose, if there are expeditions against the Malays, I shall have to go with them; but the fewer of them there are the better I shall be pleased."

The talk was more serious aft, where the doctor and first lieutenant were dining with the captain. It ended by the latter saying, "Well, Doctor, if what your friend Hassan said be true, we are likely enough to have our hands pretty full, and shall have to watch this fellow Sehi as sharply as we do his neighbors. He is not under our protection yet, and if he sends his prahus down the river to plunder on the coast, as Hassan says, he is not the sort of character likely to do us credit, and the position of a British Resident with him would be the reverse of a pleasant one. However, we must hope that he is not as black as he is painted. He has evidently put the other chiefs' backs up, and we must receive their reports of him with some doubt. However, I have no doubt that, if he turns out badly, we shall be able to give him a lesson that will be of benefit to him."

The first day's voyage up the river by no means came up to the anticipations of the midshipmen as to the country through which they were to pass. The width of the river varied from a quarter of a mile to three hundred yards; the banks on each side were lined with mangroves, presenting a dreary and monotonous aspect. Progress was slow, the steam launch going ahead and sounding the depth of water, the captain having but little faith in the assertion of the native pilot that he was perfectly acquainted with every bank and shallow. Being now the dry season, the tops of many of these shoals were dry, and numbers of alligators were lying half in and half out of the water, basking in the sun.

Several of the officers who possessed rifles amused themselves by shooting at these creatures, but it was very rarely that any attention was paid to their firing, the balls glancing off the scaly armor without the alligators appearing to be conscious of anything unusual. There was more amusement in watching how, when the swell of the steamer rushed through the shallow water and broke on the shoals, the reptiles turned and scrambled back into the river, evidently alarmed at this, to them, strange phenomenon.

"I should not care about bathing here, Davis," Harry Parkhurst remarked to the old sailor.

"You are right, sir; I would rather have a stand up fight with the Malays than trust myself for two minutes in this muddy water. Why, they are worse than sharks, sir; a shark does hoist his fin as a signal that he is cruising about, but these chaps come sneaking along underneath the water, and the first you know about them is that they have got you by the leg."

"Which is the worse, Davis, a bite from an alligator or a shark?"

"Well, as far as the bite goes, Mr. Parkhurst, the shark is the worst. He will take your leg off, or a big 'un will bite a man in two halves. The alligator don't go to work that way: he gets hold of your leg, and no doubt he mangles it a bit; but he don't bite right through the bone; he just takes hold of you and drags you down to the bottom of the river, and keeps you there until you are drowned; then he polishes you off at his leisure."

"The brutes!" Harry exclaimed, with deep emphasis. "See, the first lieutenant has hit that big fellow there in the eye or the soft skin behind the leg; anyhow, he has got it hard; look how he is roaring and lashing his tail."

"What is the best way of killing them?" Dick asked.

"I have heard, sir, that in Africa the natives bait a big hook with a lump of pork, or something of that sort; then, when an alligator has swallowed it, they haul him up, holus bolus. I should say a good plan to kill them would be with 'tricity. The last ship I was in, we had an officer of the Marine Artillery who knew about such things, and he put a big cartridge into a lump of pork, with two wires, and as soon as the shark had swallowed it he would touch a spring or something, and there would be an explosion. There was not as much fun in it as having a hook, but it was quicker, and he did not do it for sport, but because he hated the sharks. I heard say that he had had a young brother killed by one of them. He would sit there on the taffrail for hours on the lookout for them, with three or four loaded lumps of pork. Why, I have known him kill as many as a dozen in a day. I expect the best part of his pay must have gone in dynamite.

"He had a narrow escape one day; somehow the thing went wrong, and in trying to set it right he fell over the taffrail. The shark had bolted the bait, but this was not enough for his appetite, and he went straight at the officer. He had had a young ensign sitting beside him, who had often watched his work, and knew how the thing went. I was standing near at the time, and he began twisting some screws and things as cool as a cucumber, though I could see as his hand shook a bit. Well, he got it right just in time, for the shark was not half a length away from the captain, and was turning himself over for a bite, when the thing went off, and there was an end of the shark. The captain was a bit shaken up, but he made a grab at the rope, and held on to it till we lowered a boat and picked him up. He had to be got up on deck in a chair, and it was two or three days before he was himself again. When he got round he set to work again more earnestly than ever; and I believe that if we had stopped in the West Indies long enough, there would not have been a shark left in those waters."

"It was a capital plan, Davis, and if we ever take possession of these rivers, we shall have to do something of that sort to get rid of the brutes. Are the Malays afraid of them?"

"I don't know, Mr. Parkhurst, but I think they are. I had a chat with a mate I met in the Myrtle, which went home the day after we relieved them here. He had been up some of the rivers, and told me that every village had a bathing place palisaded off so that the alligators could not get at the bathers."

"Well, there is one thing—we shall have to be very careful when we are out in boats, for if we were to run upon a sunken log and knock a hole in the boat's bottom, there would not be much chance of our ever reaching the shore."

"You are about right there, sir. I aint afraid of Malays, but it gives me the creeps down my back when I think of one of them chaps getting hold of me by the leg. Bob Pearson told me that the only chance you have is to send your knife, or if you can't get at that, your thumbs, into the creature's eyes. But it would require a mighty cool hand to find the eyes, with the brute's teeth in one's leg, and the water so thick with mud that you could not see an inch beyond your nose."

"Well, I will make a note of that, anyhow, Davis, and I will take a good look at the next alligator I see dead, so as to know exactly where to feel for its eyes."

On the second day the scenery changed. In place of the mangroves a dense forest lined the river. Birds of lovely plumage occasionally flew across it, and after they had anchored in the evening, the air became full of strange noises; great beasts rose and snorted near the banks; sounds of roaring and growling were heard in the wood; and the lads, who had been so eager before to take part in a hunt on shore, listened with something like awe to the various strange and often mysterious noises.

"What in the world does it all mean, Doctor?" Dick Balderson asked, as the surgeon came up to the spot where the four midshipmen were leaning on the rail.

"It means that there is a good deal of life in the woods. That splashing sound you hear with deep grunts and snorts, is probably made by a hippopotamus wallowing in shallow water; but it may be a rhinoceros, or even a buffalo. That roar is either a tiger or a panther, and that snarling sound on the other bank is, no doubt, made by smaller animals of the same family, indulging in a domestic quarrel. Some of the other sounds are made by night birds of some kind or other and perhaps by monkeys, and I fancy that distant vibrating sound that goes on without intermission is a concert of a party of frogs."

"What is that?" as a shrill cry, as from a child, followed by a confused outburst of cries, chattering, and, as it seemed to them, a barking sound, followed.

"I fancy that is the death cry of a monkey. Probably some python or other snake has seized it in its sleep; and the other noise is the outcry of its companions heaping abuse upon the snake, but unable to do anything to rescue their friend."

"I don't think, Doctor," Harry Parkhurst said, in a tone that was half in earnest, "that I feel so anxious as I did for sport in the forest; and certainly I should decline to take part in it after nightfall."

"I can quite understand that, lad. At night all the sounds of a tropical forest seem mysterious and weird, but in the broad daylight the bush will be comparatively still. The nocturnal animals will slink away to their lairs, and there will seem nothing strange to you in the songs and calls of the birds. I should recommend you all to take a sound dose of quinine tonight; I have a two and a half gallon keg of the stuff mixed, and any officer or man can go and take a glass whenever he feels he wants it. It would be good for your nerves, as well as neutralize the effect of the damp rising from the river. I should advise you who are not on the watch to turn in early; it is of no use your exposing yourselves more than is necessary to the miasma."

The next day progress was more rapid, for the captain found that the assurance of the pilot that there was amply sufficient water for the Serpent had been verified, and he therefore steamed forward at half speed, without sending the launch on ahead to take soundings. Several villages were passed by the way, but though the inhabitants assembled on the banks and watched the steamer, no boats were put out, nor were any attempts made to barter their products with the strangers.

"It does not look as if we were popular, Mr. Ferguson," the captain said to the first lieutenant. "It may be that they object to our presence altogether, or it may be because they believe that we are going to the assistance of this Rajah Sehi. It certainly does not look well for the future."

"Not at all, sir. However, we shall be at the rajah's place tomorrow morning, and shall then have a better opportunity of seeing how things are likely to go. At any rate, he is sure to be civil for a time, and we shall be likely to procure fruit and vegetables, which, as the doctor says, are absolute necessities if the men are to be kept in good health."

The next morning they anchored about ten o'clock opposite the campong of the rajah. It was a good deal larger than any that they had passed on the way up, but the houses were mere huts, with the exception of a large wooden structure, which they at once concluded was the residence of the rajah. As soon as the Serpent turned the last bend of the river before reaching the place, the sound of drums and gongs was heard, and a large boat, manned by eighteen rowers, shot out from the bank as the anchor was dropped. The two officials on board at once mounted the accommodation ladder, and on reaching the deck were received by the first lieutenant, behind whom stood a guard of honor of the marines.

Upon stating that they came to express, on behalf of the rajah, the pleasure he felt at their arrival, they were conducted to the captain's cabin. Compliments were exchanged through the medium of the interpreter, and a bottle of champagne was opened, and its contents appeared to gratify the visitors. They announced that the rajah would receive the captain that afternoon at his palace.

CHAPTER IV

Neither of the midshipmen was present at the interview between the captain and the rajah. The second lieutenant, the captain of the marines, and the doctor alone accompanied him, with an escort of twenty bluejackets and as many marines. A large crowd of people had collected to see them pass along to the palace, which was a bare, barn-like structure, but they looked on sullenly and silently as the party passed through them on their way. They were kept waiting some little time outside the building, then entered through a doorway which led them into a large, unfurnished room, at the end of which the rajah was seated. He rose when the officers entered, and received them with an appearance of great cordiality, his chiefs standing behind him.

The conversation was wholly of a complimentary character; the subject of the business on which the British ship had come was not even touched upon; refreshments, consisting of native sweets and palm wine, were then passed round, and the captain, seeing that all business talk was to be deferred, took his leave.

The doctor, who was fond of the two midshipmen, was always ready to chat freely with them.

"What did you think of our ally, Dr. Horsley?" Dick asked him, when, having changed his full uniform for a suit of undress, he came up on deck.

"Between you and me, Balderson, I have seldom seen a more unmitigated looking ruffian in my life; even for a Malay, he is ugly. Soh Hay tells me that in his young days he was a great fighter, and his face and shoulders are seamed with scars. I asked how he came to be rajah; for he does not look at all the type of the better class of people. Soh told me that, in the first place, he took to the jungle, owing to his having krised in a quarrel the son of the chief here. He was joined by other fugitives, set up as a pirate, and captured by surprise one of the chief's prahus. His force grew rapidly, and he made a night attack on the chief's campong, killed him and all the members of his family, and caused himself to be elected chief of the tribe, which was then a small one. Gradually he swallowed up one after another of his weaker neighbors, sometimes by force, sometimes by treachery. I believe he is now confronted by more powerful chiefs, and that it is only because he is possessed of some six or eight piratical prahus that he has been able to maintain his position. No doubt he has become alarmed by a prospect of a combination against him, and has so invited us to support him. Such a step will, of course, greatly add to his unpopularity, but doubtless he thinks that, with our help, he could defy his enemies."

"But, he cannot suppose, Doctor," Harry said indignantly, "that we are going to fight for such a rascal as he is against the men he has been plundering."

"I don't expect he does think that we are going to fight for him, unless he can show us that it is to our interest to do so. I should imagine that he hopes that the effect of our appearance here will be to either induce his neighbors to come to some arrangement with him, or that he will endeavor to make peace with them by offering to throw us over, and to join with them against us."

"Then, I should say, Doctor, that the best thing would be to hang the ruffian up at once."

"Well, yes, that might be a good plan, Parkhurst," the doctor said with a smile, "and might save us a good deal of trouble; but, you see, we have come up here at his invitation; we have just been eating his food and drinking his liquor, and it would scarcely place us in a favorable position in the eyes of the natives in general were we to commence our alliance with him by hanging him."

Harry laughed. "No, I suppose not, Doctor. Still, what are we to do?"

"We must wait, lad. We are here to ascertain the precise situation, and it will be some time before that will be cleared up. Certainly for the present there will be nothing for us to do but to keep quiet and see how matters turn out, and to get through the time as best we may. We shall have fine opportunities for shooting and botanizing, for whatever the chief's designs may be, it is certain that at present he will do all in his power to please us. The captain today, at my suggestion, said that, in order to keep the men in good health, it would be desirable that they should have every opportunity of going ashore, and that the officers should make expeditions in search of game into the interior. He promised at once to afford us every facility, and to provide us with guides and beaters."

The next day permission was granted to several of the officers and to twenty sailors and a dozen marines to go on shore. Before starting, the whole ship's company were drawn up, and the captain addressed them upon the absolute necessity for good behavior.

"The Malays," he said, "are a fierce race, very proud and independent, and quick to resent the smallest insult. Each man carries a kris, and is ready to use it on the slightest provocation. Every man who goes ashore must remember that not only his own life, but those of many others, and the success of the mission on which we have come hither, may be forfeited by any careless act of aggression. Many of you have served on the coast of Africa, but you must remember that the Malays are not to be treated in the same free and easy manner that may go down with negroes. You must comport yourselves with the same decency of behavior that you would were you in the port of a friendly European Power. Any breach of these orders will be most severely punished; and I appeal to every officer and man to use his utmost efforts to keep on good terms with these people, and to behave as if the honor and credit of the ship depended upon him personally. Any man who comes on board in the slightest degree the worse for liquor will not be allowed to land again, even if we are stationed here for six months; and if there is any misbehavior on shore, all leave will be stopped."

Two days later, the captain, with the second lieutenant and doctor, again paid a visit to the rajah, and this time business matters were entered upon. The chief began by stating that he rejoiced at the thought of being under the protection of the great English Queen. The captain replied that her Majesty was anxious to be on good terms with all the Malay chiefs; that those rajahs and sultans who had accepted her protection had greatly benefited by so doing, and by listening to the advice of the officers whom she sent to reside at their seat of government; but that, of course, before receiving his state under her protection it was necessary that her representative, the Governor of the Straits Settlements, should be thoroughly satisfied that the rajah intended to be guided by the advice so given.

He said that it was thoroughly necessary this should be understood, for that the allegiance offered to the Queen could not be lightly thrown off. If a chief once owned her as his sovereign, he could not change his mind afterwards; and should he disobey the advice and orders of the Resident, he would be liable to be dethroned, and his government bestowed upon one better fitted for it. He could not, for instance, be allowed to engage in hostilities against his neighbors without the consent of the Resident, for it was clear that the English could not assist him in wars in which they considered that he was in the wrong. In these matters there must be benefits on both sides: the chief would obtain protection against warlike neighbors, would benefit by the presence and advice of a British officer, and by the trade that would spring up; while, in return for these benefits, he must acknowledge the Queen as his sovereign, and must obey the orders of her officers just as her native born subjects would do.

The chief looked very serious at this. "Cannot," he asked at last, "a chief obtain the protection of the British, and afterwards remain as an ally of theirs?"

"Not so," the captain said; "he cannot come to us when he is in danger and ask us to send ships and men to aid him, and afterwards, when the danger has passed, wish us good morning, and give us nothing in return for the benefits he had received."

"What orders would a Resident give?" the rajah asked, after a pause.

"He would give such orders as would be necessary for the good of the state; without interfering in matters of home government, he would not allow acts of tyranny and cruelty that would imperil the peace of the state, and perhaps bring about a rising. He would not suffer trade passing through the dominions to be hampered and injured by heavy and unjust exactions; although, doubtless, he would allow legitimate tolls to be taken. He would not permit expeditions to be fitted out for attacks upon harmless neighbors. His interference would always be for the good of the state, and, consequently, for the good of its prince. The incomes of the various rulers who have placed themselves under British protection have always been largely augmented by the prosperity and well doing of the state, the increase in its population, the extension of its trade and agriculture, all of which enabled the people to pay a larger amount of taxation.

"You see, Rajah, we force no one to place himself under our protection; we war with no one unless, by attack upon ourselves or upon princes under our protection, he compels us to punish him, and, in extreme cases, to take possession of his dominions. I am explaining all this to you because I wish you thoroughly to understand what your position will be if the Queen takes you under her protection—which she certainly will not do unless it is found that you are likely, on your part, to carry out faithfully the obligations you have assumed in return for that protection."

When this had been translated to the rajah by the interpreter, the chief sat for some time silent. It was evident that he was ill pleased, and that he had reckoned upon obtaining the British aid without undertaking any responsibilities whatever.

"And the officer who will come up," he said at last, "would he reside on shore?"

"Certainly he would. A portion of ground would be allotted for the Residency; on this a fort would be erected, which would be manned by a small force for his protection; and he might either reside in the fort or in a residence erected for him close to it, and under shelter of its guns. The fort would, of course, be used for the protection of the town against enemies, as well as for the protection of the officer against any rising on the part of your people; in which case you, as well as himself, would find a refuge in it."

"Then I should no longer be a ruler," the rajah said angrily. "I should not be able to order those who offended me to be punished."

"Not at all," the captain replied quietly. "Your powers as a ruler would not be interfered with in any way, as long as they were properly exercised. You would have the power of executing ill doers in accordance with the custom of your country; but the murder of a person who had committed no crime whatever is not to be permitted, and anything like wholesale cruelty and tyranny would be sternly repressed."

For some time the rajah sat without speaking; then he said, with an evident effort of self control, "I must think all this over; it is all new to me."

"By all means do so," the captain replied. "The matter is an important one, and you will do well to consider it in all lights before you take a step that, once taken, cannot be undone."

"I don't like the fellow's looks, Doctor," the captain said; "he intended to use us as a cat's paw against his neighbors."

"I think that he is a thoroughly bad lot, sir; and if he accepted the terms, I should be very sorry to be appointed Resident, for I should not feel that my life was worth a day's purchase."

"Well, there is nothing to do but to wait until we get a definite answer from him; and my instructions are that, if I find that he is not a desirable man to have to deal with, I am to enter into negotiations with other rajahs, and to endeavor to do something to open the trade of the river and to render it safe for merchants who come up to trade. If Hassan's account of this man's doings is correct, he is the main cause of the falling off in the trade, and, moreover, the author of the piracies of which we have had so many complaints; indeed, it is possible that when the Governor learns the true state of things, I may get an order to present an ultimatum to this fellow and to sink his piratical craft. At any rate, we may make up our minds to be here for some time."

On the following day a message was received from the rajah, saying that if any of the officers wished to go on excursions for sport, guides would be placed at their disposal, and that all who wished to do so could at any time travel through the country without the slightest fear of molestation. For some time affairs remained in the same condition. The doctor went daily on shore with butterfly and beetle nets, tin boxes, and other paraphernalia. He was generally accompanied by a couple of bluejackets, and always took a native guide to prevent the risk of being lost in the jungle, and also because the man was able to take him to places where villages had stood, and it was in these clearings that insect life, especially among the lepidoptera, was most abundant. The Malay he first engaged was a young fellow who proved so intelligent and willing that he was permanently retained for the service as long as the Serpent remained on the station.

The officers obtained no sport with big game; for although at night the forest was full of sounds, showing the number of wild animals that abounded, these never were met with during the daytime, and it would have been hopeless endeavoring to penetrate the thick jungle in search of them. There was, however, an abundance of birds, for the most part of brilliant plumage, and the doctor was delighted with the spoils they brought in, while the messes were kept well supplied with jungle fowl and other edible birds. The natives, learning from the guide of the doctor's passion for insects, brought in large numbers for sale, and he was able to purchase a great many specimens altogether new to science.

The two midshipmen made excursions with their guns whenever they could get leave. Davis and two other sailors always accompanied them, as the captain's orders were strict that no officer or man should go outside the limits of the campong unless accompanied by two armed seamen.

Sometimes they took a native canoe and went up the river fishing; but as an abundance of fish could be caught by lines from the ship's side, they only did this as a change, and often in the cool of the evening they lay lazily in the canoe, while the fishermen were employed rowing them up one or other of the numerous streams which flowed into the river. The doctor's prognostications as to the health of the crew were only partially verified, for the precautions taken, if they did not secure a perfect immunity against fever, at least greatly diminished the number of those who suffered from it. The abundance of fish either caught from the ship or purchased from the natives formed a wholesome diet, aided by the fruit, of which the natives brought off a very large quantity. It was very varied, and much of it delicious; the mangosteens were specially appreciated, and those who could overcome their repugnance to the disgusting odor of the durians found them delicious eating. Besides these were custard apples, bananas, and many other kinds of fruit; all were very cheap and, upon the doctor's suggestion, a supply was purchased daily for the use of the ship's company, and the sailors, who had no other use for their money, laid out no small portion of their pay on these luxuries.

The captain had taken every opportunity, when boats passed up the river, to send messages and presents to the chiefs of the tribes higher up, with assurances that he had not come up as an enemy, but that he desired to be on good terms with all, and would gladly see any of them who would come down to pay him a visit, and would guarantee their safe return without molestation on the part of Sehi. No answers had, however, been received to these overtures, and a proposal he made to the rajah to send some of the ship's boats up the river to endeavor to bring about an understanding between him and his neighbors was received with extreme disfavor.

CHAPTER V

So far, nothing had been seen of the rajah's prahus. When questioned on the subject, he replied that they were all down on the coast, trading with the natives; but it was so improbable that they should have been sent away while the rajah was in fear of an attack by his neighbors that no credence was given to the assertion. The ship's boats often went out for long rows on the river, ostensibly—as the captain told the rajah, who inquired suspiciously as to the meaning of these excursions—for the sake of giving the crews active exercise, but principally in order to take soundings of the river, and to investigate the size and positions of the creeks running into it. One day the gig and cutter had proceeded farther than usual; they had started at daybreak, and had turned off into what seemed a very small creek, that had hitherto been unexplored, as from the width of its mouth it was supposed to extend but a short distance into the forest. The master's mate was in command of one boat, the second lieutenant of the other; Harry Parkhurst accompanied the latter. After pushing through the screen of foliage that almost closed the entrance to the creek, the boats rowed on for some distance. For half a mile the width was but some fifteen yards, and the trees met in an arch overhead, then it widened considerably.

"This is just the sort of place," the lieutenant said to Harry, "where the rajah's prahus may be hidden away. We had best go along as noiselessly as possible. If we were to come upon them suddenly they might fire upon us, and that would bring on a general row. If we should catch sight of them, it would be best to take the news to the captain, and let him act as he thinks fit."

He ordered the men to cease rowing until the gig came alongside.

"Mr. Morrison," he said, "it seems to me that this is a likely place for the prahus to be hidden. We had better try and discover if this is the case, without being ourselves seen; therefore have all the oars, except four, laid in, and let the men muffle those with their stockings, and be most careful to dip them into the water without making a splash. Let absolute silence be preserved in the boat. I will lead the way as before, and if I hold up my hand stop rowing instantly."

"Aye, aye, sir!" the mate replied.

The same precautions were taken by the cutter, and the boats proceeded noiselessly. Presently the stream narrowed again, until it seemed that they were approaching its termination, and the boat stopped rowing.

"I fancy we have come to the end of it, Mr. Morrison," the lieutenant said in a low voice.

"I am afraid so too, sir; there is no room for the oars, and we shall either have to punt the boats, or to drag them by the bushes."

The lieutenant was about to give the order to turn when Harry said, suddenly, "There is a current, sir. I have had my eye upon that root, and we have drifted backwards a couple of feet since we lost way, so there must be a stretch of water above us."

The lieutenant watched the root of the tree to which Harry had pointed, for a minute in silence, then he said, "You are right, my lad, there is a current, and, as you say, there must be a stretch of water above us. Lay in your oars, lads; stand up, and pull her along by the boughs and bushes, but don't make the slightest sound."

Twenty yards farther the creek widened, and the oars were again got out.

"Take your place in the bow, Mr. Parkhurst, and hold up your hand the instant you see anything unusual, and do you, men, be ready to hold her up the instant I give the order."

They proceeded for a quarter of a mile, the gig following close behind. Suddenly, at a bend in the stream, a glare of light was seen ahead. Harry held up his hand, and passed the word down in a whisper that just ahead the creek widened into a broad sheet of water. The lieutenant stopped the gig by holding up his hand, passed the order for the men to lay in their oars noiselessly, and told the coxswain to keep in well under the bushes on the left hand side; then he made his way forward, and joined Harry, telling the men to pull the boat forward by means of the branches overhead which were well within reach, but to avoid breaking even a twig.

In a minute or two the bow of the boat arrived at the end of the screen of bushes, and a low exclamation broke from the lieutenant and Harry simultaneously; they were looking out on to an almost circular pool some two hundred yards in diameter. In the center were moored six prahus. Two of them lay broadside on to the creek, the other four were in a line behind these, and it seemed that their broadsides were directed to the opposite side of the pool, for the other two boats were in the way of their firing at the creek. They were long, low vessels, rowing some twenty oars on each side. Each carried a number of small brass guns, and they were evidently full of men, for numbers could be seen on deck, and boats were passing to and fro between them and a small village at the edge of the pool. Having taken in all the details of the scene, the lieutenant passed the word for the mate to leave his own boat and join him. When he did so, he whispered to him: "I thought it was as well that you should have a view of these fellows' position too, Morrison, as it would be of use to you if you have to take a boat in to attack them."

Two minutes later the boats were drawn back again to the open water in their rear, and rowed as noiselessly as before down the creek, no word being spoken until they were half a mile away from the pool.

"That is a snug hiding place, Mr. Morrison," the lieutenant said.

"It is indeed, sir. Who would have thought the scoundrels were so close to us, or that they lay up this narrow creek, which I have passed half a dozen times and never thought worth examining? I should not have dreamt that one of those craft could have passed through."

"I doubt whether they did pass through. They hardly could have done so without breaking down a good many of these branches, and we must have seen signs of that. I think they must have got into that pool by some creek coming in on the opposite side. You see four out of the six boats were anchored in line so as to bring their broadsides to bear on some point opposite to them, while the other two guarded them against any attack from this side. Naturally, they thought it unlikely that any boat would come up here, and so directed their main attention to the other opening. The next thing to find out will be where the other stream joins the river, otherwise, as soon as we make our appearance, they will escape that way, and there is not the least doubt that they could row away from our fastest boats. However, it is a great thing that we have discovered their whereabouts without their having the least notion that we have done so, and I am sure the captain will be very pleased when he hears that we have found them. It will give him the whip hand over that lying rascal Sehi."

Captain Forest smiled grimly when the lieutenant made his report of the discovery that he had made.

"Thank you, Mr. Hopkins; that is a very valuable discovery. Just at present matters have not come to a point when we can turn it to account. The next thing will be to find out where the other passage comes out. It will be a serious business to attack them in the boats alone; these prahus carry a tremendous lot of men, and the Malays will fight desperately. I do not say that we might not succeed, but we should lose a lot of men in the attempt; it would be hot work even with the ship, attacked by six of these fellows at once. If it was in the night, we might fail to see any of them before they were upon us, and we should have hard work to beat back four or five hundred of them if they all came swarming on deck together. However, we can wait, and the first time the rajah shows any signs of treachery we can pounce upon his fleet. He will not dream that we have discovered their hiding place, and will therefore let them hide there without movement. However, we must try to find the ether end of the entrance to the creek.

"Please impress upon Mr. Morrison and young Parkhurst that it is of the highest importance no words shall be spoken about it; and it might be advisable, also, to give notice to the men who were in the boats, to keep their mouths shut. I have no reason to believe that the interpreter is not faithful to our interests, but it is just as well not to trust anyone. Moreover, it may be that some of these Malays who come on board with fruit may have been for a time at Singapore or Penang, and picked up a little English, and a chance word might let them know that we have discovered the prahus."

"I wonder why our friend Hassan has not turned up," Dick Balderson said to his chum one day, after they had been lying for a month opposite the town.

"I expect something has occurred to keep him," Harry said. "I am quite convinced that he would have come if he could. He may be in trouble himself with some of his neighbors, or he may have tried to exert himself too soon and done himself damage. I am quite convinced that he meant what he said. At any rate, till this business here comes to a head, we are not likely to be able to go up and pay a visit to him."

"No, I am quite sure that the captain would not let us go now, and indeed, I would not ask him, even if I were sure he would, for we may get to blows with the rajah any day; he cannot put off giving a final answer much longer. I wonder the captain stood his shilly shallying so long as he has."

It was but two evenings after this that, as the two midshipmen were leaning against the bulwarks, watching the reflection of the stars in the sluggish stream, a native sampan stole silently out from the shadow of the shore and dropped down alongside the Serpent. So noiseless was the movement that the two men on the lookout in the bow did not notice it, and the midshipmen thought it was a shadow of some dark object floating down stream, when it came alongside and a man stood up.

"Hello!" Harry said, "you must not come alongside like this: what do you want?"

"Dick, Harry, Doctor; come from Hassan."

"Oh, that is it; all right, come on board," and, leaning over, he stretched out his hand to the native, who seized it, and in a moment stood by his side on the deck, holding the head rope of his sampan in his mouth.

"Davis," Harry said to the sailor who was standing two paces away, "just go down to the wardroom, and tell the doctor, with my compliments, that I shall be obliged if he will come on deck at once. Say that it is something particular."

A minute later the doctor appeared. "I was just in the middle of a rubber, Dick, and if you have not an uncommonly good reason for calling me up I will make you smart for it, the first time you get under my hands. Whom have we got here?"

"He is a messenger from Hassan; he mentioned our names and yours."

"Ah, I am glad of that," the doctor said, rubbing his hands together; "they have been chaffing me in the wardroom about it, and prophesying that I should never hear of him again. Well, what does he say?"

"He has not said anything except our names, Doctor, and that he comes from Hassan. I don't suppose he knows any more English, and I thought we had better consult you, whether it would be best to send for Soh Hay; he may have brought some message of importance."

"Right, lad. I think the most prudent thing will be to tell the captain first. It may only be a message to say why he has not come, or it may be a matter of some importance. I will go to him at once."

Two or three minutes later he returned. "You are to bring him to the captain's cabin. Here, Davis, pass the word forward that the captain wants to see Soh Hay in his cabin."

Harry touched the native, who had been standing quietly by his side, and signed him to accompany them, and with Dr. Horsley and Dick went direct to the cabin.

"So your friend has sent a message at last, lad?" Captain Forest said. "I am glad of that, for I own that I had doubts whether we should hear any more of him."

"You come from the chief Hassan?" the captain, who had been working at the Malay language, with the interpreter, since he had arrived at the mouth of the river, asked in that tongue. The man's face brightened.

"Yes, my lord," he said.

"Is he well?"

"The chief is quite well."

"I wish I knew enough to question him without Soh Hay's interference, but I shall only make a mess of it, and, perhaps, get a wrong idea altogether of his message. Now, Soh Hay," he broke off as the interpreter entered, "you will ask this man the questions exactly as I put them, and tell me his answer word for word. It may be of importance. Now ask him first what message he brings from his chief to the officers."

Among Malay Pirates

The question was put, and the native, speaking slowly and quietly, and evidently repeating a lesson that he had learned by heart, said, "The chief sends his greeting to his three friends, Harry, Dick, and Doctor, also to Captain. He is well in body; he is cured, and can throw a spear and lead his men to battle. He has sent four messengers one after another, but none have returned with an answer; they have no doubt been krised. Now he sends me."

"Tell him that no messenger has arrived until now," the captain said, when this was interpreted to him.

The man nodded. "All krised. I travel at night, hide in trees all day, float down at night in shadow of bushes, and have got through safe. Chief Hassan says not been able to come down. Other chiefs very angry because English warship come. Send message to Hassan to join them. When he say no, they threaten to kill him and destroy tribe when warship go away. Two of Rajah Sehi's prahus go up and down river; stop all boats. Sehi send message to all chiefs; say that English war boat here. English come take his country, and after they done that take the countries of the others; make themselves kings of the river. He ask them to join him in killing English, every man, then he would have no more quarrel with them, no trouble trade any more; be good friends with all neighbors. Some chiefs say one thing, some another. Some more afraid of rajah than of English; some think better have English here than rajah.

"Hassan says must take great care. Sehi very treacherous; attack when they do not expect it. He thinks his prahus can easily take English ship; but Hassan says Sehi wants the other chiefs to aid, so that if the English send up more ships, then, can all join him in fighting them. Hassan says he will do what he can. He has eight war canoes, but no good against prahus—they run at canoes, and cut them in half; but will come to help if English attack. He does not know where prahus are. Begs Captain to attack these first; it is they that make Sehi master of the river. If they destroyed, other chiefs not afraid of Sehi, and he might get some of them to join against him. Hassan said tell Harry, and Dick, and Doctor he does not forget their kindness, and will do what he can to watch over them. Such is Hassan's message."

"Ask him when he is going back to his chief," the captain said.

"He go now," the interpreter said, after asking the question. "He get as far as he can before morning. He sure many eyes watch ship night and day to see that no message comes, or any word of what rajah is doing. He float down stream in sampan some distance, then paddle to opposite bank, then keep in shadow of bushes up the river, and hide away till night comes again."

"Very well, then, tell him that he is to thank his master for sending us warning; that we had already found out that what he told us before he went away was true, and that Sehi is a very bad man. Say that we are not afraid of prahus, and will make short work of them when we get a chance. Tell him we will take great care, and not let ourselves be surprised, and that when we have finished with this fellow here, the ship will come as far up the river as she can go, and show the chiefs that the English have no evil intentions against them, and will send his three friends with a strong boat party to pay him a visit. By the way, ask the man if he knows this part of the country."

"Yes, Captain; he says that he has been since his boyhood a boatman, and has worked for some years with a trader, who used to go up the creeks, and trade with the villagers."

"Ask him if he knows a creek that turns off from the river four or five miles above this; it is a very small one, but it leads into a pool on which is a large village."

The man nodded at once, when the question was put, then spoke for a minute or two.

"He says, Captain, that he knows the pool and village; but he has never been up the small creek that you speak of. Did not know that a boat could get through. He has been there by a large creek that runs into the other branch of the river, the one that turns off twelve miles below this; from that river it is an hour's paddle in a sampan to the pool."

"How should we know the entrance?" the captain asked.

"Entrance difficult to find," the native replied; "strip of land runs out from both sides, covered with trees. One goes a little beyond the other, so that anyone who did not know it would pass the entrance without noticing it. It is just wide enough for a large craft to go in and out. There is a village stands a hundred yards below the entrance; it would be known by a big tree that grows before a large house close to the bank. The water is deep on that side. You have only, after passing the village, to keep close in shore, and you will then see the entrance to the creek. It is called Alligator Creek, because, more than any place, it swarms with these creatures."

"Thank you," the captain said. "Will you tell the chief that I say you have rendered me a valuable service?"

He opened a case in which he kept presents intended for the chiefs, and took out a brace of handsome pistols, a powder flask, and a bullet mold.

"Take these," he said, "in token of the service you have rendered. When I see your chief, you shall be well recompensed for the risk that you have run in bearing me his message."

The Malay looked longingly at the pistols, and then said, "I came by order of my chief, and not for reward."

"Quite so. I understand that, and am not offering you a reward for that service, but for the information that you have given me, which may be of value if I have trouble with the rajah here."

The man bowed and took the pistols offered. "I will use them against your enemies," he said warmly; "but all of us know the creek, for it is that which renders it so difficult for us to fight against Sehi. He is master of the water, and we cannot attack him without first crossing that creek. We should have to carry canoes with us, to do it, for the creek is too full of alligators for anyone to swim across, and our small canoes would have no chance of passing the creek when his war boats were there."

The captain nodded when this was translated to him.

"Sehi's place, in fact, stands upon an island formed by the two branches of the river and this creek. As soon as he became master of the river, he could hardly be assailed, while at any time he could sally out and fall upon his enemies. Ask the man if he will take any refreshment before he goes."

The man declined. He had, he said, sufficient fruit and dried fish for his journey back. A few minutes later he took his place in the little canoe and drifted away into the darkness, and was soon lost to sight.

CHAPTER VI

"Things are coming to a crisis, Harry," Dick Balderson said, in a tone of delight, as they left the captain's cabin. "We now know what we all along suspected—the rajah is a rascal, and we have not only found out where his prahus are hidden, but have them corked up in a bottle."

"Nothing could be better, Dick, and I expect we shall have some pretty hot work. Of course the Serpent cannot get up that creek, though she can place herself at the entrance and prevent their getting away; but there still remains the work of capturing or driving them down the creek, and that is likely to be a very tough job."

The next morning the second lieutenant, the mate, and Harry Parkhurst were sent for to the captain's cabin. The first lieutenant was there. They were each asked their opinion as to whether the prahus could force their way through the creek by which they had ascended.

"It is a most important point," the captain said: "and indeed, everything might depend upon it."

"I am sure, sir," Mr. Hopkins said, "that they could not go straight down it. They might cut their way through, but it would be a work of considerable time, for with their masts they would have to clear away the branches to a considerable height. Down near the water the branches by which we pushed ourselves along were those of the undergrowth, with many rattans and other creepers varying from the thickness of one's thumb to that of one's wrist, and these would take a great deal of chopping before one of their war boats could be pushed through, but higher up they would probably have much thicker branches to contend with. It may be that they can lower their masts; but even if they could do so, I should think that it would take them over an hour's work, even with the number of hands they carry, to get a passage through that bit of thick undergrowth, fifty or sixty yards up the mouth of the creek. There are two or three other places where some chopping would have to be done, but that would be comparatively easy work."

The mate and Harry both agreed with the lieutenant.

"Practically, then," the captain said, "the Malays have but one mode of escape, while we have two of attack. At any rate, if we send up a boat beforehand, and fasten two or three iron chains from side to side among the branches, that passage would be securely sealed.

"Thank you, gentlemen; that is all I have to ask at present. It is a very difficult nut we have to crack, Mr. Ferguson," he went on, when he and the first lieutenant were alone. "To attack six strongly armed prahus with the boats of this ship would be a serious enterprise indeed, and its success would be very doubtful, while the loss would certainly be very heavy, especially as, if any of the boats were sunk, the crews would have but little chance in a place swarming with alligators. I don't think I should be justified in risking such an enterprise."

"There is no doubt, sir, the loss would be very heavy indeed; by all accounts, these Malays fight like demons on the decks of their own boats, and, for aught we know, they may, after nightfall, trice up rattans to prevent boarders getting on board. I have heard that it is their custom when they expect an attack, and that these are far more formidable obstacles than our boarding nets. Of course I should be quite ready to lead an attack should you decide upon making one, but I cannot conceal from myself that it would be a well nigh desperate undertaking."

"I am glad that you are of that opinion," the captain said. "There seems to me but one course, and that a difficult one—namely, to carry a couple of heavy guns through the forest to the edge of the pool. It would be a serious undertaking, and we should have to send a strong force to defend them, but if we could succeed in planting them in position, we should soon drive the Malays out of the pool."

"That would be a capital plan, Captain, if it could be managed. I suppose before we attempt it, you will take possession of this place, and capture the rajah?"

"That of course. I don't suppose we shall capture him. I have no doubt that we are closely watched night and day, and that the instant the boats are lowered, and the men get on board, the rajah would prepare for flight, though he might possibly make some resistance. However, that would be but trifling; our guns would cover the landing, and knock the place about his ears; but to penetrate the jungle would be vastly more difficult an affair. If, as is probable, he has succeeded in inducing some of his neighbors to join him, they may have already sent strong contingents, and the forest may be full of them. In that case it would be quite beyond our power to rout them out, and I certainly should not be justified in attempting it. The destruction of his town and the burning of his palace would be a serious blow to him, but the destruction of his piratical fleet would be a very much heavier one. If we can achieve that, we shall have done good service.

"The first thing to do is to find out whether there is a path either from this river, or the other branch, to the pool. If so, at dark, after destroying the town, we will recall all the men on shore, buoy the anchor and drop it noiselessly, and drift down the river till we are far enough away to use the engines, then steam down to the junction of the two streams, and up again to the entrance to the creek on that side. Then we will at once land a very strong party, land also two twenty-four pounders, and drag them to the pool. We might hope to do so without any opposition, for the Malays would no doubt be gathered at the edge of the forest near the town to repel any attack we might make from there, and before morning we might have the guns in position. I should take a hundred empty sacks. These you would fill with earth when you get near the pool, and form a battery with them behind the screen of bushes; then, when you are ready, you will cut down the bushes and open fire."

"I don't see why that should not succeed, sir. Of course the most difficult part of the operation is dragging the guns. These native paths are only broad enough for men in single file."

"Yes, that is the difficulty. We could not employ axes to cut down the trees, and to saw them down would be an interminable work. I think, Mr. Ferguson, we should have to carry them."

"I doubt if we could carry a twenty-four pounder, sir; but we might carry an eighteen. They have bamboos of almost any length here, and if we were to lash an eighteen pounder between two of them, I should say that ten men each side ought to able to carry them, while as many more might take the gun carriage."

"We will get some bamboos today, Mr. Ferguson, and try the experiment of how many men will be required to carry a gun; but now I think of it, I fancy that it will be still easier to lay the guns down on a sledge shaped piece of timber—these paths are smooth enough where the natives tread, and the men could haul the guns along with ropes."

"That would be better and easier, sir. The difficulty with the carriages will be greatest, but they might be taken to pieces as far as possible and slung on bamboos."

"I think that we shall be able to manage all that," the captain said cheerfully. "The first thing is to find the path. There is almost sure to be one from the village the Malay spoke of as close to the mouth of the creek, and the pool, and if we send the boats up as soon as we arrive at the creek, to row with muffled oars until they get near the pool, and then land and find the path, it would diminish very much the distance they would have to go and the work to be done."

"It would be a great thing to find that out beforehand, sir. If you like, I will drop down the river this afternoon in the gig; that will attract no attention, for it will be thought that we are merely going fishing or shooting. As soon as it is dark we will muffle the oars, and row up the other branch, find the mouth of the creek and row up it, first find how far it is to the pool, then drop down a quarter of a mile and land, strike into the jungle, and look for the path. I should, of course, choose a point where the creek bends that way, for as the path no doubt goes straight from the village to the pool, it would be nearer the creek at a bend than it would be at any other point. If it is a sharp bend it might go quite close to it."

"That would be a very good plan, Mr. Ferguson, and as you have proposed it, you shall take command of the boat; otherwise I should have sent either the third lieutenant or Morrison. I need not say that it will be necessary to use the greatest caution, and to avoid all risks as much as possible, though I fancy that my gig would run away from any of the ordinary native craft; but, of course, the great point is to avoid being noticed, for were one of our boats seen up the other river near the creek, the alarm would be given, and the prahus might at once shift their position, and make up the river, where we should have little chance of finding them again."

"I quite understand that, sir, and will be as careful as possible. I will take one of the midshipmen with me, either Mr. Parkhurst or Mr. Balderson; if the worst came to the worst and one of the men were hit, he could man his oar, or, if I were myself badly wounded, could take the command. I think it is Balderson's turn for boat duty."

"Either of them will do," the captain said; "they are both strong, active lads, and as steady as you can expect lads to be."

Accordingly, at four in the afternoon the captain's gig was lowered. As the rule was that all men on boat duty should go armed no surprise had been excited when the order was given for the men to take their muskets and cutlasses, though, when an extra supply of ammunition and a brace of pistols were served out to each, they thought that something unusual was in the wind, and there was a grin on the men's faces when a hamper of provisions was placed in the bow of the boat. Dick was in a state of high but suppressed delight when informed by the first lieutenant that he was to accompany him on a boat expedition, and that he had better take his cloak with him, as they might be out all night.

"You can take your pistols with you, Mr. Balderson; it is not likely that they will be wanted, but it is as well to carry them."

Dick borrowed a cutlass from the armorer and ground it down to a razor edge, for his dirk was an altogether useless weapon if it came to fighting. He was the more convinced that something more than usual was intended when he saw the assistant surgeon place a parcel in the stern sheets.

"Bandages, I expect," he said. "Where do you think we can be going, Harry?"

"Perhaps you are going up the creek again, Dick. Who's going in command?"

"I have not heard. Morrison says he has not been told off, so I suppose it is Hopkins; in fact, if you are going up the creek, it is sure to be him, as one of us who went up there before would certainly be in command. It is rum they're taking the captain's gig. He is very particular about it, and it is very seldom indeed that even the first luff uses it."

"I suppose they think it possible that you may be chased, and there is no doubt she is far away the fastest boat on board. She is not a dockyard boat, but, as you know, is one the captain had specially built for himself, and for racing if we were at any station where there were other warships."

When four o'clock came, and the first lieutenant, with his cloak over his arm, came out and took his place in the boat, there was a general look of surprise among the sailors leaning on the rail to see her put off, for it was a very unusual thing for the first officer to take the command when only a single boat's crew were going out on any expedition.

"Row easy, men," Mr. Ferguson said, as he sat down on one side of the coxswain, while Dick took his place on the other. "Drop quietly down the river. There is my fishing rod by your side, Mr. Balderson; you may as well begin to put it together at once, so that the natives on shore may see that we are going on a fishing expedition."

They rowed some ten miles down at a leisurely pace, and then the boat's grapnel was dropped at a bend of the stream, where the water was unusually deep, and several baskets of fish had been taken at various times. A spare rod was brought out from under the seat, and Mr. Ferguson and Dick began to fish, one on each side of the boat, while the men lay on their oars, and a look of satisfaction came over their faces as the lieutenant told them that they could smoke. Hitherto, Dick had been in ignorance as to the object of the expedition. He had been much surprised when the order had been given for the boat to row down the river, and it was therefore evident that it was not the intention of the first officer to again explore the creek.

Several fish were caught, but as soon as it became dark the lieutenant said, "You can throw them overboard again, Mr. Balderson; we don't want any extra weight in the boat, and these fish must weigh thirty pounds at least. Now what do you suppose we are going to do?"

"I have no idea, sir. I thought that we might be going up the creek that Lieutenant Hopkins explored the other day, to have another look at the prahus; but as we came down the river instead of going up, of course it is not that."

"No; we are going to explore the creek, but from the other end."

"That will be first rate, sir, but I am afraid that we shan't find water enough for the Serpent."

"No, I fear that there is little chance of that; still we may obtain information that will be valuable."

The night was a dark one, and an hour after sunset the grapnel was got up, and the boat continued its way down the river, the oars being now muffled, and the strictest silence ordered.

"Keep your eyes open, Mr. Balderson," the lieutenant said. "I think that it must be another three miles to the point where the river forks. The other branch comes in on the right, so we will keep on the left bank. I don't think there is much fear of our missing the junction of the stream, but if we do, we will row on to a mile below the point where we think it is, then cross and keep up on the other side. In that way we cannot miss it."

For the next half hour no word was spoken in the boat. Dick kept his eyes fixed on the opposite bank. Suddenly he touched the lieutenant.

"There, sir, that must be it. The line of the trees has suddenly stopped, and I think I can make out a lower line behind it."

"Yes, no doubt that is the junction. We will go two hundred yards farther down before we cross; it is unlikely in the extreme that anyone is watching us, still I don't want to run the slightest risk."

In another five minutes they crossed the river, whose increased width showed them that they had assuredly passed the junction of the stream. Then they turned and followed the right hand bank.

"Stretch out a bit now, lads; you have fifteen miles' straight rowing before you, and the sooner you get to the other end, the better. We may have a long night's work before us, and I want to be able to get to the place where we fished before morning."

The men bent to their oars, and the boat sped swiftly along. The current was very slight, and after two hours' rowing, the lieutenant judged that they must be but a short distance from the village Hassan's messenger spoke of. Accordingly, he told the coxswain to steer across to the other bank, and warned the men that the slightest splash of their oars might attract attention, and that they were to row easier for the present. In a quarter of an hour the wall of forest ceased, and a hundred yards farther they saw houses. Two or three dim lights were visible, and the sound of voices could be heard. The boat's head was now turned out somewhat farther into the stream, so as to be out of sight of anyone who might by chance come down late to draw water. After rowing a hundred yards they could dimly make out the outline of a white house. There was a break just in the center, and the outline of a tree could be seen above the roof. Dick leant forward and again touched the lieutenant.

"That must be the house, sir," he whispered.

Mr. Ferguson nodded without speaking; and after the boat had gone another hundred yards, the line of forest could again be seen, and the boat was rowed into the bank, and two minutes later shot through a narrow channel and entered a creek some forty yards wide.

"Now you can give way again, lads."

An hour's paddling in a sampan would mean about three miles, and after twenty minutes' sharp rowing, the men were ordered to row easy again, and the lieutenant and Dick kept an anxious lookout ahead. The creek was here little more than fifty yards across, and, accustomed as their eyes were to darkness, they presently saw that it widened out suddenly. The word was passed down for the men to paddle easily, and in two minutes the pool opened before them. They could not make out the prahus, lying as they did against the shadow of the trees on the farther side, but they could see a number of lights, apparently from swinging lanterns, and hear a loud murmur of voices.

"Easy all," the lieutenant ordered now; "back her very quietly; now pull bow."

Noiselessly the boat was brought round, and its head directed to the right hand bank. They had passed a sharp bend nearly half a mile back, and the lieutenant said, "Look out for a landing place at the deepest point of the curve, Harris."

"Aye, aye, sir!" the coxswain said, standing up. A minute later he brought the boat alongside, at a point which was free from bushes, and where the bank was but two feet above the water's edge.

CHAPTER VII

"Now, Mr. Balderson, take Harper and Winthorpe, and make your way through the jungle as noiselessly as possible. It is probable that the path runs within fifty yards of this point, possibly it is only half a dozen. When you have found it, send Winthorpe back to me with the news. Take that long coil of thin rope that is in the bow, and pay it out as you go along. You might get lost even within two yards of the stream, and it would be dangerous to call or whistle. It will enable me to join you. Leave your muskets behind, lads; they would only be in the way in the jungle, and you have your pistols and cutlasses. You take the lantern, Winthorpe, and Harper, do you take the rope. Fasten one end to the thwart before you start, or, without knowing it, you might drag it after you."

Dick led the way, the others following close behind, but as soon as they were among the trees, he was obliged to take the lantern, for the darkness was so intense that he could not see an inch before him and would have been torn to pieces by the thorny creepers had he tried to penetrate without a light.

As it was, he received several nasty scratches, and could hear muttered exclamations from the men behind him. Creeping under some of the rattans, making detours to avoid others, and cutting some of the smaller ones in two with his cutlass, he made his way forward, and was delighted indeed when, after proceeding some twenty yards, he came upon the edge of what looked like a ditch, but which was, he knew, the native path.

"Here we are, lads," he exclaimed in a low tone; "thank goodness we have not had to go farther."

"So say I, sir," one of the men grumbled; "if it had not been for your lantern I should have been torn to pieces. As it is, I aint sure whether my eyes aint gone, and my nose and cheeks are scratched as if I had been fighting with a mad cat."

"Here, Winthorpe, take the lantern and make your way back; darken it as soon as you get through to the edge of the creek. You cannot go wrong with the cord to guide you."

Two or three minutes later Dick saw the light approaching again, and the lieutenant, the coxswain, and two bluejackets joined him, Winthorpe and another having been left as boat keepers.

"Now, Harris, do you and one of the others go on ahead; we will follow fifty yards behind you. If you hear anyone coming, give a low whistle; we will then turn off the light. You can walk on confidently, for there is no chance of any of these prickly creepers running across the path. When you see the trees are getting thinner, or that there is an opening before you, stop and send back word to us, so that we can shut up the lantern before joining you."

The lieutenant headed the party now, followed by Dick. He held the lantern close to the ground; the bottom was, like all jungle paths, worn perfectly smooth by the passage of the barefooted natives.

"Nothing could be better," he said in a low voice to Dick. "We ought to be able to haul the guns along here at a trot; and the opening is wide enough on each side for a gun carriage to be carried along without any difficulty."

In ten minutes one of the men ahead came back.

"We have got to the end of the path, sir; it ends on the bank of that pool we saw ahead."

The lantern was now extinguished, and the party hurried forward. On reaching the bank they found that the path ended, as they had expected, just opposite the village. The prahus lay somewhat to the right.

"It could not be better," the lieutenant whispered. "Now let us see whether we can find a suitable place for the guns."

This was much easier than they had expected, for the trees were cleared, probably to furnish firewood, for a distance of some fifteen yards from the bank; between this cleared place and the water was a fringe of thick bushes.

"This will do capitally, lads. Now we will be off at once; we have found out all that we wanted, and nothing could be more satisfactory."

They retraced their steps rapidly till they came to the coil of cord looped on a low bough. The coxswain took it down, and they were soon all on board the boat again. "Now, lads, row as noiselessly as you can to the mouth of the pool again, then turn, and lay on your oars, except bow and two, who are to paddle very slowly. Hand Mr. Balderson that twenty foot bamboo; I want to sound the river as we come back."

As soon as the boat was again turned, Dick took the pole, and, standing up, thrust it down into the water.

"Only about seven feet, sir," he whispered.

"That is bad. It is evident that the ship cannot get up here; still we may as well go on sounding."

"The water is gradually deepening," Dick said, thrusting the pole down again; "there are nearly ten feet."

It was not long before he announced fifteen, and at that continued until they reached the entrance to the creek, where it was only fourteen feet.

"It would be a touch and go there," the lieutenant said, "but I dare say she could be pushed through. It is very unfortunate that there is that shallow bar this side of the pool. And now, lads, you can lay out for ten minutes, and then we can fasten up to a bough and see what is in the hamper. We have done our work earlier than I had expected, and can take it easy."

The steward had provided them with an ample store of food, and the men ate their hunks of cold meat and bread, and passed round the pannikins of grog, with great contentment, while the officers divided a cold chicken and a bottle of claret.

"Now, men," the lieutenant said, when they had finished, "you can have a quarter of an hour's smoke. You must open the lantern in the bottom of the boat, and hold a jacket over it to prevent the light falling on any of you."

When the men had lit their pipes the lantern was passed aft, and while the coxswain put his jacket over it, the lieutenant lit a cigar.

"You smoke, don't you, Balderson?"

"Yes, sir, I began when we came up the river; the doctor said it is a good thing to keep off miasma."

"Very well, then light up; I think that it is a good thing myself. We have done a very satisfactory night's work, and I think we see our way now to getting rid of most of those piratical craft, which will not only be a benefit to traders on the coast of the river, but will greatly please all the other chiefs, and will enable them to hold their own against Sehi."

Five minutes were added to the promised quarter, and then the pipes were laid down, and the boat proceeded at a steady stroke until they reached the spot where they had fished.

"Somewhere about here, lad?"

"Yes, sir, I think that this is just the place. I noticed that tall tree rising above the general line just opposite where we were anchored."

"Then lower the grapnel; in oars."

Another bottle was produced from the hamper; the lieutenant filled a wine glass full and drank it off, and then passed the glass over to Dick.

"What is it, sir?"

"It is some grog, with a large dose of quinine. The doctor begged me to give it an hour or two before daylight. Now, lads, you are each to take a glass of this; it will protect you against the effect of the mist on the river. You can show the lantern now; it is just as well that they should see it if they are on the lookout."

Every man took his glass of the mixture.

"Now wrap yourselves in your blankets, lads, and lie down for a couple of hours' sleep."

After a minute or two's scuffling while each found a plank to suit him, all was quiet in the boat. Dick, who felt far too excited over the events of the night to be sleepy, had volunteered to keep watch, and, lighting another pipe at the lantern, smoked till it was broad daylight. Then he roused the crew, and in less than two hours afterwards they rowed alongside the Serpent. The captain was greatly pleased with Mr. Ferguson's report.

"It is unlucky about that bar in the creek, otherwise we might have taken the ship right into the pool, and fought it out with them there. Still, it may be that this will be the best in the end, for we could hardly have counted upon sinking the whole of them, and once past us they would have been off like the wind; and though we might have followed some of them, the others would have made off, some one way and some another, whereas, by laying the vessel across the mouth of the creek, we have a good chance of catching them all as they come down. There is no doubt a lot more fellows have arrived to help the rajah; we can see that there are a great many more about on the shore than there have been before. I think things will come to a crisis before many hours have passed. We have made out that men keep coming and going behind that row of six huts facing the river, and I should not be surprised if they are not hard at work establishing a battery there."

Presently two Malays, whom they recognized as belonging to the rajah's council, advanced to the edge of the shore, which was but some fifty yards away. One of them held a pole to which a white cloth was attached.

"I have a message from the rajah," he shouted out. The captain sent for the interpreter, and went to the side of the quarterdeck.

"The rajah says that he does not want to have any more to say to you. You want to take his country; he will not let you have it, and if you do not go away in an hour, he will sink your ship."

"Tell him," the captain said, "that it will be the worse for him if he tries it. I came up here at his invitation, and shall stay just as long as I please."

The two Malays retired, walking in a quiet and dignified way.

The news soon ran through the ship of the defiance that had been given, and excited the liveliest satisfaction. The men were shaking hands, cutting capers, and indulging in much joking and laughter. Half an hour later there was a sudden uproar in the town, drums were beaten, horns sounded, and the Malays by the river bank speedily retired behind the huts.

"You had better get the magazine opened, Mr. Ferguson, and everything in readiness, but we won't beat to quarters till they begin."

The tumult on shore increased, and soon a few shots were fired from behind houses and walls, the balls whistling overhead.

"There won't be much of that," the captain said, as he walked up and down the quarterdeck with the first lieutenant; "we have seen very few guns among them. I should doubt if there are a hundred in the town. What there are were, no doubt, captured from trading vessels the scoundrels have plundered and burned."

A few minutes later the bamboos forming the wall of the six houses where a bustle had been observed fell outward, the lashings having been cut by a swarm of Malays, who, as soon as the last fell, ran back, showing eight brass cannon.

"Beat to quarters, Mr. Ferguson," the Captain said quietly, and at the first tap of the drum the sailors, who had been expecting the order, ran to their stations. As they gained them the little battery on shore opened fire. Although the distance was but a hundred yards, only three of the balls hit the hull, the others passing through the masts.

"Load with grape," the captain ordered.

"Captain Hugeson," he said to the Marine officer, "will you place your men on the poop, and tell them to open fire as soon as the guns send the Malays flying from their battery? I can see that there are large numbers gathered round it. Mr. Ferguson, will you see that the guns are all laid on that battery? When they are ready, fire a broadside that will clear the place out at once."

Two minutes later there was a crash as the whole of the guns on the starboard side were discharged at the same moment. The effect was tremendous, and the storm of grape swept away the whole of the buildings beneath which the guns were standing. Three of these were dismounted, and not one of the men who had been crowded round them remained on his feet. Numbers were seen running away in all directions, and a volley from the marines brought several of these down.

"There is an end to the attack," the captain said quietly. "Order the men to load with shell, and to direct their aim in the first place at the rajah's palace; there is no occasion for rapid firing."

Gun after gun sent its messenger into the palace, and in three or four minutes flames were seen rising from it. The order was then given to fire with grape at all the houses facing the water. In the meantime the men were called from their guns on the port side, and the boats lowered. The marines and all the sailors, save those serving the starboard guns, took their places in them, the first lieutenant taking the command, and on the word being given they dashed with a cheer towards the shore, and, leaping out, formed up, and led by their officers ran forward, not a shot being fired by the Malays as they did so.

The fire of the ship's guns was now directed towards the portion of the town facing the forest, as it was here that the Malays would probably be gathered. Port fires had been distributed among the landing party. As these were lost to sight as they entered the town, those on board ship watched eagerly for the sound of combat. Nothing, however, was heard for a minute or two; then came a single shot, and then a rattle of musketry.

"They are making a stand now," the captain said.

"Mr. Hopkins, will you please go round and tell the gunners to be very careful in their aim? Let them watch the smoke rising among the houses, and aim a short distance beyond it. Impress upon them that it is better to fire too far than to risk hurting our own men."

The order was obeyed; soon flames were seen to rise beyond the spot where the fighting was going on, the resistance to the advance speedily ceased, and a dropping fire took the place of the sustained roll of musketry which, five minutes later, broke out again at the edge of the town facing the wood, and the fire of the guns was now directed against the edge of the forest, to which the Malays had evidently fled. In a few minutes smoke began to rise all round the place, showing that the men with port fires were at work, and in a quarter of an hour the bluejackets and marines were seen issuing from the houses and coming down to the shore. The place was by this time a sheet of fire, the lightly built huts, dried in the heat of the sun, catching like tinder, and blazing up in a fierce flame, that in a few minutes left no vestige behind it.

The ship's fire had by this time ceased, and the sailors, as they looked out of the portholes, cheered as the boats came up. Their appearance was far less orderly than it had been when they put off from the ship, every man having carted off some sort of loot—sarongs, spears, krises, and other articles, some obtained from the huts, others thrown away by the Malays in their flight. There were, too, some articles of European manufacture, which had been carried off from the palace before the flames had obtained entire possession. These were in themselves strong proofs that the rajah's prahus had been engaged in piratical attacks upon European craft, for they consisted of bales of silk, chronometers, watches, double barreled guns, mirrors, and other articles which had evidently formed a portion of a ship's fittings.

"Any casualties, Mr. Ferguson?" the captain asked, as the lieutenant stepped on board.

"Half a dozen spear wounds, sir, but only one of a serious nature; our fire was too hot for them to face."

"What do you suppose their loss has been?"

Among Malay Pirates

"As far as I can judge, sir, some eighty or ninety were killed by our fire, and at least as many must have fallen in the battery; the place was choked up with dead. I have brought the eight guns off; they are only four pounders."

"They may be useful for the boats. I see the men have brought off a good deal of rubbish. You had better give orders that whatever there is is to be fairly divided among all hands. Any articles more valuable than the rest had better be put up to auction, and whatever they fetch also divided among the men. Were the Malays in force?"

"The place swarmed with them, sir, but they were evidently demoralized by the fire of the guns, and their attacks were really feeble. The only trouble we had was that some would shut themselves up in houses. It looked at first as if they really meant to fight, but directly the shells began to fall behind them, and fire broke out, they lost heart altogether, and made a bolt for the forest."

"Well, the work has been thoroughly done, Mr. Ferguson, and Sehi has had a lesson that he won't forget. Now we have to tackle his fleet."

"Everything is ready, sir. We have got the sledges made for the two guns, and a store of long bamboos for the carriages and anything else we may want to take with us."

"This will be a more serious business by a long way," the captain said. "The men had better take a hundred rounds of ammunition with them, and it would be as well to take a few boxes of spare cartridges; and the men not occupied in dragging the cannon and carrying the carriages, must take up as many rounds of shell as possible, and eight or ten rounds of grape for each gun. You have got the sacks ready for forming the battery; that will be absolutely necessary for the protection of the men firing. Each of the prahus has probably got at least half a dozen small guns, and it would be hardly possible to work our pieces unless the men were protected from their concentrated fire. Tell the chief engineer that steam must be got up by six o'clock. In the meantime, let a slow fire be kept up towards the edge of the forest, just a shot every five minutes, which will be enough to show them we are still here, and have not done with them yet. When the place cools down a bit, we will send a party on shore to keep up a dropping fire against the forest, and so induce them to believe that we mean to attack them there."

CHAPTER VIII

During the rest of the day preparations were actively carried on for the night's work. The fifty marines and a hundred bluejackets were to take part in the landing expedition; the ammunition to be carried was ranged along the deck, and the men told off for the various work there was to be done, some being allotted to carry stretchers and surgical requirements for the wounded. The first lieutenant was to command the party, having with him the third lieutenant, the master's mate, and the two senior midshipmen; besides, of course, the marine officers. Dr. Horsley was also to accompany them. Some cartridges were made up with powder and musket bullets for two of the brass guns captured, in order that, if the Malays succeeded in landing, they might meet with a hot reception. It was decided that no carriages should be taken for them, but that they should be simply laid on the sandbags.

The party on shore had kept up a fire all day at the forest. The yells of defiance which at times rose showed that the Malays were in great force all round its edge. Towards evening all on shore returned to the ship. As soon as it became absolutely dark, the anchor chain was unshackled, and a buoy being attached to the end, it was noiselessly lowered into the water. Then the screw began to revolve, and the vessel gradually backed down the river. All lights had been extinguished, and no sound from the forest showed that the movement had been observed. A mile lower down the ship was turned, the screw began to revolve more rapidly, and at half speed she ran down to the junction of the two branches of the river, and steamed up the other arm until within half a mile or so of the village at the mouth of the creek. Then a light anchor was let go, the boats were lowered, and the landing party took their places in them; the oars were all muffled, and keeping close to the right bank of the river, they rowed up until past the village, and then crossing, entered the mouth of the creek, and rowed up it until they reached the spot where the landing had been effected on the previous night.

Half a dozen men provided with well greased saws first landed under Dick Balderson's command, and cleared a passage six feet wide to the path; then the landing began in earnest. The guns were first put on shore, and carried bodily to the path; the rest of the marines and the bluejackets then landed, each carrying, in addition to his arms and ammunition, a gun cartridge, or a box of rifle ammunition, and a couple of empty sacks. As fast as they landed they proceeded up the path. Dick Balderson led the way, and the men were directed to step as closely as they could to each other. As they arrived near the pool, each deposited his burden, and then went back to assist to drag up the guns and carriages.

Scarcely a sound was heard during the operation. Their feet fell noiselessly on the soft earth of the track, and no one a few yards away would have guessed that a hundred and fifty men were engaged in laborious toil. There was far more noise than there had been the night before on board the prahus, an incessant jabber being maintained, and voices rang high in excitement as the men discussed the destruction of the town and the orders that had been received for a portion of them to land on the following morning and take part in the annihilation of the whites if they entered into the forest. As soon as the two heavy guns were placed upon their carriages, just behind the screen of bushes, the greater portion of the men were sent back as far as the point where they had landed, there to fill the sacks with earth from the bank of the river, a number of shovels having been brought for the purpose.

Several large bundles of bamboos, cut into lengths six feet long, and sharpened at both ends, had been among the articles taken up to the battery, and while most of the men were engaged filling and carrying the sacks of earth, some were employed in constructing chevaux de frise, ten paces on each side of the spot where the battery was being constructed. The bamboos were set diagonally a foot and a half into the soft earth, and bound together by being lashed to strong poles running along them. These fences extended from the edge of the bushes by the water to the trees. The forest behind was so thick and entangled with creepers that there was little fear of an attack being made from that quarter.

Accustomed to work in the darkness, the sailors had no difficulty in carrying out the operation, and before morning broke the battery was complete. It was six feet high on the side facing the water, with two embrasures for the guns, four feet high on the sides covered by the chevaux de frise. The front face was twenty-five feet in length, the sides forty. Morning was breaking as the work was finished, and bread and cold meat were served out, with a full ration of grog. By the time these were consumed it was broad daylight; for there is little twilight so near the equator.

"Now for it, Dick," Harry Parkhurst said, as the lieutenant gave the signal for all to rise and take their places. Filing out of the battery, the marines lined the bank on one side, and the sailors, other than those who were to work the guns, on the other. Some of the sailors climbed over the front wall and with their jackknives cut away the boughs in front of the guns. There was silence on board the prahus, where the Malays had dropped off to sleep a couple of hours before daylight. Mr. Ferguson himself superintended the laying of the guns, seeing that each was most carefully trained upon the waterline of a prahu. As the distance was some seventy or eighty yards, he had little doubt that the two vessels aimed at would be sunk at once. When he was thoroughly satisfied, he drew back and gave the order to fire.

The two reports sounded as if one, and were mingled with the explosion of shells as they struck the prahus exactly on the waterline. There was a momentary silence, and then a wild hubbub of yells of surprise and fury, while a loud cheer broke from the British, as they saw the success of the shots. Almost instantly the two craft struck began to settle down, and in a minute disappeared, the water being covered with the heads of the crew, who were swimming to the other prahus. The guns of these had evidently been kept loaded, for before the two eighteen pounders were again ready, a fire was opened by the four craft, one or two balls striking the sandbags, while the rest went crashing into the forest behind. Every shot from the British guns struck the prahus, but none effected such damage as the first two fired.

G. A. Henty

"They are taking to their boats, Ferguson," the doctor, who was standing beside him, said.

"Yes, but I fancy they have no thought of giving it up at present; they are going to make a dash at us. They can still work their guns and spare any amount of men to attack us."

The next minute, indeed, a dozen boats, crammed with men, shot round from behind the prahus.

"Grape now," the lieutenant ordered, while, at the same moment, the marines and seamen, who had hitherto been silent, opened fire from under the bushes, beneath which they were enabled to obtain a view of what was going on.

Two of the boats were sunk by the discharge of the grape; but the others, without checking their course, pushed on.

"Quick, lads, give them another round before it is too late."

The guns were loaded with incredible quickness, and two more of the boats were shattered, their swarthy occupants striking out for the shore, making for the most part towards the battery, as did the boats. Twenty of the sailors and as many marines were at once called in from the bank to aid in the defense of the battery, and a desperate conflict was presently raging here and along the bank, the Malays, swarming up, striving to force their way up through the embrasures, or to climb the sandbags; but as fast as they did so, they were cut down or bayoneted by its defenders. Those trying to land at other points were impeded by the bushes, and numbers were killed; but they pressed on so furiously that at last Mr. Ferguson, who had been moving backwards and forwards along the line, thought it best to call the men in, and in a minute or two the whole party were collected in the little fort, and ranged along the sides.

With furious yells the Malays came on, and although swept by volleys of musketry reached the bamboos, which they strove in vain to pluck up or climb. In the meantime the eighteen pounders had never ceased their fire, the sailors working them steadily, regardless of the fight that was going on on either flank. Here the little brass guns did good service; each time they were fired the recoil sent them tumbling from the top of the sandbags, only, however, to be seized, sponged, and loaded, by the four sailors in charge of each, and then lifted to their place again, crammed with bullets to the muzzle, in readiness to check the next charge of the Malays. Suddenly their yells redoubled, and were answered by similar shouts from the forest.

"The rajah's troops have come up," the first lieutenant said to the marine officer; "our position is getting serious. Do you think that we could make our way back to the boats without great loss? We have sunk two of their craft, have badly damaged the others, and inflicted very heavy loss on them."

"It would be a very risky operation; but it might be done, Ferguson. Listen!"

There was a fresh outburst of shouts, this time on the path by which they had come. Evidently a number of the newly arrived Malays had struck into it by some other track from the town.

"That settles it," the lieutenant said shortly; "we must fight it out here. It is lucky we have a fair stock of ammunition, and can keep it up for some hours yet.

You see, the sailors have not had to use their pistols yet, and they will astonish those fellows if they do manage to scale the sandbags."

For another half hour the fighting continued. Again and again the Malays fell back, but only to return to the attack with fresh fury, and the defenders had been obliged to betake themselves more than once to their pistols. The two heavy guns were now removed from their position to the sides, for the attack by boats had ceased entirely, and the destruction of the prahus was of less importance than the defense of the little fort from the attacks on its flanks. The operation began just as the Malays made one of their retreats, and by the time they returned, the guns were placed in their new position, their muzzles peeping out from among the sandbags, while the embrasures on the water face had been closed by bags taken from the upper line. The effect of the fire at such close quarters was to drive the Malays flying into the forest. Shortly afterwards the sound of chopping was heard.

"The beggars are trying to cut a path through the jungle to our rear, Dick," Harry Parkhurst said.

"Obstinate brutes! But I don't think much of that, Harry: they will get on well enough until they arrive within twenty or thirty yards of us, when we can pepper them so hotly that they will soon get sick of it."

At this moment there was the report of a heavy gun, and a shell crashed through the forest fifty yards in the rear of the fort. Loud yells of rage and alarm rose from the Malays, while a hearty cheer broke from the defenders of the fort. Closely following, came the sound of another gun, and then a rain of grape, some of which whistled over the fort.

"Keep yourselves well down behind the sandbags, men," Lieutenant Ferguson shouted; "the captain knows that we have shelter, and will sweep the Malays out of the forest round us. That shot must have done great execution among the Malays on the path between us and the boats."

The guns of the ship kept up a heavy fire, searching the wood for some distance round with shell, and pouring volleys of grape into the trees near the battery. Presently the fire ceased.

"I fancy they have all bolted, Dick," his comrade said; "after the first five minutes we have not heard a sound. I wonder what the prahus are doing?"

A minute later the lieutenant said, "Mr. Morrison, take a dozen men and make your way along the path until you get to the boats. I hope they have escaped. If they are within hail go on board, and report to the captain that we have sunk two of the prahus, and that for the present the Malays who have been attacking us have made off. Say that large numbers of them have gone on board the four prahus, and that I am about to open fire upon them again."

As soon as the mate had left, parties of men were set to work to shift the guns to their old positions, and fire was again opened upon the piratical prahus, who replied, as before, with their little guns. A very few minutes later a shell flew overhead, and fell in the water near where the craft were anchored. Another and another followed quickly. Intense excitement was manifest on board the prahus, and almost immediately their cables were cut, oars got out, and at a great rate they started down the creek.

"The place has got too hot for them altogether, Harry; they think it better to run the gauntlet of the ship's guns than to be sunk at their moorings."

Scarcely had the prahus issued from the pool, than the guns of the ship were heard.

"I am afraid that some of them will get away, Harry. The beggars row so fast that there won't be time to give them more than one broadside as they pass. If the ship is aground, which is likely enough, for the captain pushed up farther than we thought possible, they will be pretty safe when they have once got past her."

Presently the guns were heard to fire in rapid succession. Loud yells and cries followed; then came shouts of triumph and defiance; then all was still, save that a few cannon shot were discharged at regular intervals.

"They have got one of the guns round to fire over the stern, Dick. There, it has stopped now; evidently the prahus have got round the next corner. It is a pity that any of them should have escaped, and they would not have done so if the Serpent had remained at the mouth of the creek; but I suppose the captain became anxious at the continuation of the heavy firing here, and so came up to our help. It is lucky he did so, for, though we might have beaten them off, they were in such tremendous force that I fancy it would have gone hard with us in the long run. I was beginning to think so myself, Harry."

Dr. Horsley had been busy enough from the time that the fighting began in earnest. Ten men had been killed by balls that had passed through the embrasures, or by kris or lance wounds, and twenty-eight others had been more or less severely wounded. A quarter of an hour after the firing ceased, Captain Forrest himself, with the mate, rowed into the pool in one of the cutters, and landed at the end of the path close to the battery.

"I congratulate you on your success, Mr. Ferguson," he said, shaking hands with the first lieutenant; "it has been a very hot affair, and by Mr. Morrison's report it was just as well that I decided to change my plan and come up to your aid, though it has resulted in two of the prahus getting away."

"Then you sank two of them, sir?"

"No, indeed, we only sank one; the third went down just after we saw her come out from the pool. Certainly we had not hit her, so that the honor of accounting for three out of six of the craft falls to you and your party. Well, Doctor, what is your report? I am afraid it is a bad one."

"Serious, indeed," he went on, after he had received the figures. "Still it is much less than might have been expected from attacking such a host of pirates. I am glad to hear that none of the officers are dangerously wounded."

"Parkhurst had his forearm laid open with a cut from a kris, and Balderson had one of their spears through his ear. Dr. Horsley said if it had been half an inch more to the left, it would probably have killed him. Lieutenant Somers of the marines is more badly hurt, a spear having gone through the thigh. It cut an artery. Luckily the doctor was close to him at the moment, and clapped on a tourniquet, and then cut down to the artery and tied it. As he says, 'A delay of two minutes, and it would have been all up with the young fellow.' Are the boats safe, sir?"

"Yes, the boat keepers pushed off a little way when the firing began in the forest, and when they heard the shouts of a large party of the enemy coming along the path, they went out almost into the middle of the creek; and it was well they did, for many of the Malays came down through the path you cut, and would have riddled them with their spears had they been within reach. The boat keepers acted very wisely; all of them got into the gig and towed the other boats astern, so that if the Malays came along, either in their prahus or in their boats, they could have cut them adrift and made a race of it down to the ship.

"Well, I think that there is nothing more to be done here. The men may as well have a tot of grog served out, and then the sailors can march down to the landing place and bring up the boats and take the guns and what ammunition you have left, on board. Mr. Morrison will go back with me to the ship; he has one of his arms broken by a ball from the prahus."

"I did not know that he was wounded, sir; he did not report it. I should not have sent him if I had known it."

"It is just as well as it is, Ferguson; it will give me an opportunity of specially recommending him for promotion in my report. The assistant surgeon temporarily bandaged his arm when he reached the ship."

"Is she afloat, sir?"

"No; I want you back as soon as possible. We shall have to get out the anchors and heave on them. We put on a full head of steam and drove her two or three hundred yards through the mud before she finally brought up. I wanted to get as near to you as possible, in order to clear the woods round you."

By two o'clock the whole ship's company were on board again, and set to work to get her off; but it was not until after some hours' exertion that the Serpent was again afloat. She was at once turned round, steamed down to the mouth of the creek, and cast anchor opposite the village.

CHAPTER IX

The party landed at the village the next morning, but found it entirely deserted.

"It is most important that we should take a prisoner, Ferguson," the captain said, as he and the first lieutenant paced up and down the quarterdeck; "we must catch the two prahus if we can. At present we don't know whether they have gone up or down the river, and it would be absolutely useless for us to wait until we get some clew to their whereabouts. After we have finished with them, we will go up the other branch, and try to find the two we know to be up there. I should not like to leave our work unfinished."

"Certainly not, sir. I am afraid, though, it is of no use landing to try to get hold of a prisoner. No doubt the woods are full of them. There are the townspeople and those who came to help them; and though many of those who tried to swim ashore from the sunken boats may have been taken by the alligators, still the greater portion must have landed all right."

"I should think, Mr. Ferguson, that it would be a good plan to send a party of twenty men on shore after nightfall and to distribute them, two men to a hut. Possibly two or three of the Malays may come down to the village before morning, either to fetch valuables they may have left behind, or to see whether we are still here. They may come tonight, or they may come some time tomorrow, crawling through the plantations behind the houses. At any rate, I will wait here a day or two on the chance."

"Whom shall I send with the men, sir?"

"You had better send Parkhurst and Balderson; they will have more authority among the men than the younger midshipmen. The men better take three days' cooked provisions on shore and ten small kegs of water, one for each hut. I will give Parkhurst his instructions before he lands."

"Now, Mr. Parkhurst," he said, when the boat was lowered soon after dark, "you must bear in mind that the greatest vigilance will be necessary. Choose ten huts close together. One man in each hut must be always awake; there must be no talking above a whisper; and during the daytime no one must leave his hut on any account whatever. After nightfall you and Mr. Balderson will move from hut to hut, to see that a vigilant watch is kept. You must, of course, take watch and watch, night and day. You must remember that not only is it most important that a native should be captured, but you must be on your guard against an attack on yourselves. It is quite conceivable that a party may come down to see if there are any of us in the village.

"In case of attack, you must gather in one hut, and fire three shots as a signal to us; a musket shot will be fired in return. When you hear it, every man must throw himself down, for the guns will be already loaded with grape, and I shall fire a broadside towards the spot where I have heard your signal.

"As soon as the broadside is fired, make down to the shore, occupy a house close to the water, and keep the Malays off till the boats come ashore to fetch you off. Your crew has been very carefully picked. I have consulted the warrant officers, and they have selected the most taciturn men in the ship. There is to be no smoking; of course the men can chew as much as they like; but the smell of tobacco smoke would at once deter any native from entering a hut. If a Malay should come in and try to escape, he must be fired on as he runs away; but the men are to aim at his legs."

The instructions were carried out. A small hole was bored in the back of each of the huts, so that a constant watch could be kept up unseen by the closest observer in the forest, a hundred yards behind. The night passed off quietly, as did the next day. The men slept and watched by turns. On the afternoon of the second day, a native was seen moving cautiously from tree to tree along the edge of the forest. As soon as it was dark, Dick, whose watch it was, crawled cautiously from hut to hut.

"That fellow we saw today may come at any moment," he said. "If one of you see him coming, the other must place himself close to the door, and if he enters, throw himself upon him and hold his arms tightly till the others come up to help. Keep your rope handy to twist round him, and remember these fellows are as slippery as eels."

Having made the round, he returned to the hut in the center of the others that he and Harry occupied. Half an hour later, they heard a sudden outcry from the hut next to them, and rushing in, found the two men there struggling with a Malay. With their aid he was speedily bound; then the men were called from the other huts, and the whole party ran down to the water's edge, where Harry hailed the ship. A boat put off at once, and they were taken on board. The prisoner was led to the captain's cabin, and there examined through the medium of the interpreter. He refused to answer any questions until, by the captain's orders, he was taken on deck again and a noose placed round his neck, and the interpreter told him that, unless he spoke, he was to be hauled up to the yard's arm. The man was still silent.

"Tighten the strain very gradually," the captain said to the sailors holding the other end of the rope. "Raise him two or three feet above the deck, and then, when the doctor holds up his hand, lower him at once again."

This was done. The man, though half strangled, was still conscious, and on the noose being loosened, and Soh Hay saying that, unless he spoke, he would be again run up, he said, as soon as he got his breath, that he would answer any question. On being taken to the cabin, he said that the prahus had gone down the river, and had ascended the other arm. They had only gone a few miles above the town, for one had been so injured that there had been difficulty in keeping her afloat, and it was necessary to run her into a creek in order to repair her before going up farther.

Half an hour later steam was up, and before morning the Serpent lay off the mouth of the creek which the Malay pointed out as the one that the prahu had entered. The second officer was this time placed in command of the boats, he himself going in the launch, the third officer took the first cutter, the two midshipmen the second. No time was lost in making preparations, for it was desirable to capture the prahu before she was aware that the Serpent had left her position in the other river. For a mile the boats rowed up the creek, which narrowed until they were obliged to go in single file. It widened suddenly, and as the launch dashed through, a shower of balls tore up the water round her; while at the same moment a great tree fell across the creek, completely barring their retreat, and narrowly shaving the stern of the midshipmen's boat, which was the last in the line. Fortunately the launch had escaped serious injury, and with a shout of "Treachery," Lieutenant Hopkins drew his pistol to put a ball through the head of their guide, but as he did so, the man sprang overboard and dived towards the shore.

"Row, men; we have all our work cut out for us. There are three prahus ahead; steer for the center one, coxswain."

With a cheer the men bent to their oars, and dashed at the prahu which, as was evident by patches of plank freshly fastened to her side, was one of those that had before escaped them.

"Follow me," the lieutenant shouted to the boat behind; "we must take them one by one." The three boats dashed at the pirate craft, which was crowded with men, regardless of the fire from the other two vessels. The launch steered for her stem, the first cutter for her bow, while the midshipmen swept round her, and boarded her on the opposite side. A furious contest took place on her deck, the Malays being so confused by being assailed at three points simultaneously that the midshipmen's party were enabled to gain a footing with but very slight resistance. The shouts of the Malays near them brought many running from the other points, and the parties there gained a footing with comparatively little loss. Then a desperate struggle began; but the Malays were unable to withstand the furious attack of the British, and ere long began to leap overboard and swim to the other craft, which were both coming to their aid.

The launch's gun had not been fired, and, calling to Dick, Harry leaped down into the boat. The two midshipmen trained the gun upon the nearest prahu, and aiming at the waterline, fired it when the craft was within twenty feet of them. A moment later its impetus brought it against the side of the launch, which was crushed like an eggshell between it and the captured prahu, the two midshipmen springing on board just in time. It was the Malays' turn to board now, that of the British to prevent them; the musketry of the sailors and marines for a time kept the enemy off, but they strove desperately to gain a footing on board, until a loud cry was heard, and the craft into which the midshipmen had fired sank suddenly, and a loud cheer broke from the British.

The two midshipmen were engaged with the other pirate, from whom a cry of dismay arose at seeing the disappearance of their friends.

"Now, lads, follow me," Harry shouted as the Malays strove to push their craft away. Followed by a dozen sailors, they leaped on to her deck; but the efforts of the Malays succeeded in thrusting the vessels apart. In vain the midshipmen and their followers fought desperately. Harry was felled by a blow with a war club, Dick cut down with a kris; half the seamen were killed, the others jumped overboard and swam back to their vessel. Lieutenant Hopkins shouted to the men to take to the boats, and the two cutters were speedily manned. One, however, was in a sinking condition; but Lieutenant Hopkins with the other started in pursuit of the prahu, whose crew had already got their oars out, and in spite of the efforts of the sailors, soon left them behind. Pursuit was evidently hopeless, and reluctantly the lieutenant ordered the men to row back.

On returning to the scene of combat, they saw sunk near the bank the fourth of the prahus. "The spy was so far right," the second lieutenant muttered—"this fellow did sink; now we must see that she does no more mischief." He brought the captured prahu alongside the others, whose decks were but a foot or two below the water, and fired several shots through their bottoms. Then he set the captured craft on fire and took to the boats, which with great difficulty forced their way under the fallen tree and rowed back to the ship.

The third lieutenant had been shot dead, twelve men had been killed, ten of the midshipmen's party were missing, and of the rest but few had escaped without wounds more or less serious.

Harry was the first to recover his senses, being roughly brought to by a bucket of water being dashed over him. He looked round the deck. Of those who had sprung on board with him, none were visible save Dick Balderson, who was lying near him, with a cloth tightly bound round his shoulder.

As he rose into a sitting position a murmur of satisfaction broke from some Malays standing near. It was some time before he could rally his senses.

"I suppose," he thought at last, "they are either keeping us for torture or as hostages. The rajah may have given orders that any officers captured were to be spared and brought to him. I don't know what his expectations are," he muttered to himself; "but if he expects to be reinstated as rajah, and perhaps compensated for the loss of his palace, he is likely to be mistaken; and in that case it will go mighty hard with us, for there is no shadow of doubt that he is a savage and cruel brute."

He had now shaken off the numbness caused by the blow that he had received, and he managed to stagger to where Dick was lying, and knelt beside him and begged the Malays to bring water. They had evidently received orders to do all they could to revive the two young officers, and one at once brought half a gourd full. Harry had already assured himself that his friend's heart still beat. He began by pouring some water between his lips. It was not necessary to pour any over his head, for he had already received the same treatment as himself.

"Dick, old chap," he said sharply and earnestly.

The sound was evidently heard and understood, for Dick started slightly, opened his eyes and murmured, "It's not time to turn out yet?"

"You are not in your hammock, Dick; you have been wounded, and we are both prisoners in the hands of these Malays. Try and pull yourself together, but don't move; they have put a sort of bandage round your shoulder, and I am going to try and improve it."

"What is the matter with my shoulder?" Dick murmured.

"Chopped with a kris, old man. Now I am going to turn you on your side, and then cut the sleeve off the jacket. Take another drink of water; then we will set about it."

Dick did as he was ordered, and was evidently coming back to consciousness, for he looked round, and then said, "Where are the other fellows?"

"I don't know what has become of them. I think I went down before you did. However, here we are alone. Now I am going to begin."

He cut off the sleeve of the jacket and shirt at the shoulder, ripped open the seam to the neck, first taking off the rough bandage.

"It's a nasty cut, old man," he said, "but nothing dangerous, I should say. I fancy it has gone clean through the shoulder bone, and there is no doubt that it will knit again, as Hassan's did, if they do but give you time."

He rolled the shirt sleeve into a pad, saturated it with water, and laid it on the wound.

"You see I know all about it, Dick," he said cheerily, "from having watched the doctor at work on Hassan. Now I will tear this cloth into strips."

He first placed a strip of the cloth over the shoulder, crossed it under the arm, and then took the ends of the bandage across the chest and back, and tied them under his other arm. He repeated this process with half a dozen other strips; then he placed Dick's hand upon his chest, tied some of the other strips together, and bound them tightly round the arm and body, so that no movement of the limb was possible. One of the Malay's knelt down and gave him his assistance, and nodded approvingly when he had finished; then he helped Harry raise him into a sitting position against the bulwark.

"That is better," Dick said, "as far as it goes. How was it these fellows did not kill us at once?"

"I expect the rajah has ordered that all officers who may fall into their hands are to be kept as hostages, so that he can open negotiations with the skipper. If he gets what he wants, he hands us back; if not, there is no manner of doubt that he will put us out of the way without compunction."

The men were still working at the oars, and for four hours rowed without intermission through a labyrinth of creeks. At last they stopped before a small village, tied the prahu up to a tree, and then the man who seemed to be the captain went ashore with two or three others. The lads heard a loud outburst of anger, and a voice which they recognized as that of the rajah storming and raging for some time; then the hubbub ceased. An hour later the rajah himself came on board with two or three attendants, and a man whom they recognized as speaking a certain amount of English. The rajah scowled at them, and from the manner in which he kept fingering his kris they saw that it needed a great effort on his part to abstain from killing them at once. He spoke for some time in his own language, and the interpreter translated it.

"You are dogs—you and all your countrymen. The rajah is sending a message to your captain to tell him that he must build up his palace again, pay him for the warships that he has destroyed, and provide him with a guard against his enemies until a fresh fleet has been built. If he refuses to do this, you will both be killed."

"Tell him," Harry said, "that if we are dogs, anyhow we have shown him that we can bite. As to what he says, it is for the captain to answer; but I do not think that he will grant the terms, though possibly he may consent to spare the rajah's life, and to go away with his ship, if we are sent back to him without injury."

The rajah uttered a scornful exclamation. "I have six thousand men," he said, "and I do not need to beg my life; for were there twenty ships instead of one they could never find me, and not a man who landed and tried to come through the country would return alive. I have given your captain the chance. If, at the end of three days, an answer does not come granting my command, you will be krised. Keep a strict watch upon them, Captain, and kill them at once if they try to escape."

"I will guard them safely, Rajah," the captain, who, from the rich materials of his sarong and jacket, was evidently himself a chief, said quietly; "but as to escape, where could they go? They could but wander in the jungle until they died."

By night both lads felt more themselves. They had been well supplied with food, and though Harry's head ached until, as he said, it was splitting, and Dick's wound smarted severely, they were able to discuss their position. They at once agreed that escape was impossible, and would be even were they well and strong and could manage to obtain possession of a sampan, for they would but lose themselves in the labyrinth of creeks, and would, moreover, be certain to be overtaken by the native boats that would be sent off in all directions after them.

"There is nothing to do but to wait for the captain's answer," Dick said at last.

"We know what that will be," Harry said. "He will tell the chief that it would be impossible for him to grant his commands, but that he is ready to pay a certain sum for our release; that if harm comes to us, he will make peace with the chiefs who have assisted Sehi against us, on condition of their hunting him down and sending him alive or dead to the ships. But the rascal knows that he could hide himself in these swamps for a month, and he will proceed to chop off our heads without a moment's delay. We must keep our eyes open tomorrow, and endeavor to get hold of a couple of weapons. It is a deal better to die fighting than it is to have our throats cut like sheep."

CHAPTER X

The next two days passed quietly. The lads were both a great deal better, and agreed that if—which would almost certainly not be the case—a means of escape should present itself, they would seize the chance, however hopeless it might be, for that at worst they could but be cut down in attempting it. No chance, however, presented itself. Two Malays always squatted near them, and their eyes followed every movement.

"Some time tomorrow the messenger will return," Harry said. "It is clear to me that our only chance is to escape before morning. Those fellows will be watchful till the night is nearly over. Now, I propose that, just before the first gleam of daylight, we throw ourselves upon them suddenly, seize their krises, and cut them down, then leap on shore, and dash into the jungle. The night will be as dark as pitch, what with there being no moon and with the mist from the swamps. At any rate, we might get out of sight before the Malays knew what had happened. We could either go straight into the jungle and crawl into the thick bushes, and lie there until morning, and then make our start, or, what would, I think, be even better, take to the water, wade along under the bank till we reach one of those sampans fifty yards away, get in, and manage to paddle it noiselessly across to the opposite side, lift the craft out of the water, and hide it among the bushes, and then be off."

"The worst of it is the alligators, Harry."

"Yes, but we must risk that. We shall have the krises, and if they seize either of us, the other must go down and try and jab his kris into the beast's eyes. I know it is a frightfully dangerous business, and the chances are one hundred to one against our succeeding; but there is just a chance, and there is no chance at all if we leave it until tomorrow. Of course, if we succeed in getting over to the other side, we must wait close to the water until daylight. We should tear ourselves to pieces if we tried to make through the jungle in the dark."

"I tell you what would give us a better chance—we might take off two or three yards of that bandage of yours, cut the strip in half, and twist it into a rope; then when those fellows doze off a little, we might throw the things round their necks, and it would be all up with them."

"But you see I have only one arm, Harry."

"Bother it! I never thought of that. Well, I might do the securing, one fellow first, and then the other. You could get close to him, and if he moves, catch up his kris and cut him down."

"Yes, I could do that. Well, anyhow, Harry, we can but try; anything is better than waiting here hour after hour for the messenger to come back with what will be our death warrant."

They agreed to keep awake by turns, and accordingly lay down as soon as it became dark, the Malays, as usual, squatting at a distance of a couple of paces each side of them. It was about two o'clock in the morning when Dick, who was awake, saw, as he supposed, one of the crew standing up a few yards away; he was not sure, for just at that moment the figure disappeared.

"What on earth could that fellow want to stand up for and lie down again? for I can swear he was not there half a minute ago. There is another farther on." He pinched himself to make sure that he was awake. Figure after figure seemed to flit along the deck and disappear. One of the guard rose and stretched his arms; put a fresh bit of some herb that he was chewing into his mouth; moved close to the prisoners to see if they were asleep; and then resumed his former position. During the time that he was on his feet, Dick noticed that the phenomenon which had so puzzled him ceased. A quarter of an hour later it began again. He touched Harry, keeping his hand on his lips as a warning to be silent. Suddenly a wild yell broke on the still air, and in an instant the deck was alive with men; and as the two Malay watchers rose to their feet, both were cut down.

There were sounds of heavy blows, screams and yells, a short and confused struggle, and the fall of heavy bodies, while from the little village there were also sounds of conflict. The midshipmen had started to their feet, half bewildered at the sudden and desperate struggle, when a hand was laid on each of their shoulders, and a voice said, "English friends, Hassan has come."

The revulsion of feeling was so great that, for a minute, neither could speak; then Dick said, "Chief, we thank you with all our hearts. Tomorrow we should have been killed."

The chief shook hands with them both warmly, having seen that mode of salutation on board ship.

"Hassan glad," he said. "Hassan watch all time; no let Sehi kill friends. Friends save Hassan's child; he save them."

Torches were now lighted. The deck was thickly encumbered with dead; for every one of the crew of the prahu had been killed.

"Sehi killed too," the chief said, "come and see." He swung himself on shore; the boys followed his example, two of the Malays helping Dick down. They went to the village, where a number of Malays were moving about; torches had been brought from the ship, and a score of these soon lit up the scene. Two of the rajah's men had been killed outside their huts, but the majority had fallen inside. The chief asked a question of one of his followers, who pointed to a hut.

This they entered, and by the light of the torches saw the rajah lying dead upon the ground. Hassan said something to one of his men, who, with a single blow, chopped off the rajah's head.

"Send to chiefs," Hassan said. "If not see, not think dead. Much afraid of him. When know he dead, not fight any more; make peace quick."

One of the men asked a question, and the lads' limited knowledge of the language was sufficient to tell them that he was asking whether they should fire the village. Hassan shook his head. "Many men," he said, waving his arm to the forest, "see fire; come fight. Plenty of fight been; no need for more." For a time he stood with them in front of the pool. A series of splashes in the water told what was going on. The prahu was being cleared of its load of dead bodies; then several men filled buckets with water, and handed them up to the deck. The boys knew that an attempt was being made to wash away the blood. The process was repeated a dozen times. While this was going on, the pool was agitated in every direction. The lads shuddered as they looked, and remembered that they had proposed to wade along the edge. The place swarmed with alligators, who scrambled and fought for the bodies thrown over, until the number was so great that all were satisfied, and the pool became comparatively quiet, although fresh monsters, guided by the smell of blood, kept arriving on the scene.

At last the chief said, "Come," and together they returned to the prahu. The morning was now breaking, and but few signs remained of the terrible conflict of the night. At the chief's order, a large basket of wine, that had been found in the rajah's hut, was brought on board, together with another, full of bananas and other fruit.

"Well," Harry said, laughing, "we little thought, when we saw the champagne handed over to the rajah, that we were going to have the serving of it."

Hassan joined them at the meal. He had been given wine regularly by the doctor, and although he had evinced no partiality for it, but had taken it simply at the doctor's orders, he now drank a little to keep the others company. In a short time the whole of the chief's followers were gathered on deck, and the boys saw that they were no more numerous than the prahu's crew, and that it was only the advantage of surprise that had enabled them to overcome so easily both those on board the prahu and the rajah's followers in the village. The oars were got out, and the prahu proceeded up the creek, in the opposite direction to which it had entered it. "Going to ship?" Harry asked, pointing forward.

Hassan shook his head. "Going home," he said. "Sent messenger sampan tell captain both safe. Sehi killed, prahu taken. Must go home. Others angry because Hassan not join. May come and fight Hassan. Ask captain bring ship up river; messenger show channel, tell how far can go, then come in boats, hold great meeting, make peace."

The lads were well satisfied. They had a longing to see Hassan's home, and, perhaps, to do some shooting; and they thought that a few days' holiday before rejoining would be by no means unpleasant. They wished, however, that they had known that the sampan was leaving, so that they could have written a line to the captain, saying what had taken place, and that they could not rejoin. There was at first some splashing of the oars, for many of Hassan's men had had no prior experience except with sampans and large canoes. However, it was not long before they fell into the swing, and the boat proceeded at a rapid pace. Several times, as they went, natives appeared on the bank in considerable numbers, and receiving no answer to their hails, sent showers of lances. Harry, however, with the aid of two or three Malays, soon loaded the guns of the prahu.

"No kill," Hassan said. "We want make friends. No good kill."

Accordingly the guns were fired far over the heads of the assailants, who at once took to the bushes. After three hours' rowing they entered the river, and continued their course up it until long into the night, for the rowers were as anxious as was Hassan himself to reach their village. They were numerous enough to furnish relays at the oars, and the stroke never flagged until, an hour before midnight, fires were seen burning ahead, as they turned a bend of the river. The Malays raised a yell of triumph, which was answered from the village, and in a few minutes the prahu was brought up to the bank. A crowd, composed mostly of women and children, received them with shouts of welcome and gladness. Hassan at once led the midshipmen to a large hut that had evidently been prepared in readiness for them. Piles of skins lay in two of the corners, and the lads, who were utterly worn out, threw themselves down, and were almost instantly asleep.

The sun was high when the mat at the entrance was drawn aside, and Hassan entered, followed by four of his followers. One carried a great water jar and two calabashes, with some cotton cloths and towels; the other brought fruit of several varieties, eggs, and sweetmeats, together with a large gourd full of steaming coffee.

"Hassan come again," the chief said, and left the hut with his followers. The lads poured calabashes of water over each other, and felt wonderfully refreshed by their wash, which was accomplished without damage to the floor, which was of bamboos raised two feet above the ground. When they were dressed they fell to at their breakfast, and then went out of doors. Hassan had evidently been watching for them, for he came out of his house, which was next to that which they occupied, holding his little girl's hand. She at once ran up to them, saluting them by their names.

"Bahi very glad to see you," she said, "very glad to see good, kind officers." The child had picked up, during her month on board the ship, a great deal of English, from her constant communication with the officers and crew.

"Bad men wound Dick," she went on pitifully. "Wicked men to hurt him."

"Bahi, will you tell your father how much we are obliged to him for having come to our rescue. We should have been killed if he had not come."

The child translated the sentence. The chief smiled.

"Tell them," he said, "that Hassan is glad to have been able to pay back a little of the obligation he was under to them. Besides, Sehi Pandash was my enemy. Good thing to help friends and kill enemy at the same time. Tell them that Hassan does not want thanks; they did not like him to thank them for saving you."

The child translated this with some difficulty. Then he led the midshipmen round the village, and showed them the strong palisade which had evidently just been erected, and explained, through the child, that it had only been built before he left, as but fifteen men were available for guarding the place in his absence.

The next four days were spent in shooting expeditions, and although they met with no wild beasts, they secured a large number of bird skins for the doctor. On the fifth day a native ran in and said that boats with white men were coming. The midshipmen ran down to the bank, and saw the ship's two cutters and a gig approaching. The captain himself was in the stern of the latter, and the doctor was sitting beside him. A minute or two later they were shaking hands with the officers, and saying a few words to the men, who were evidently delighted to see them again. Just as the greetings were over, Hassan, in a rich silk sarong and jacket, came down towards them. He was leading his little daughter, and six Malays followed them.

"Welcome, Captain," he said gravely. "Hassan very glad to see you. All come right now."

"Thank you, chief. We have learned from your messenger how gallantly you have rescued my two officers, and put an end to our troubles by killing the Rajah Sehi, and capturing the last of the piratical craft."

This was too much for Hassan, and had to be translated by Soh Hay. Since the chief's return, a number of his men had been occupied in constructing bamboo huts for the use of the captain, officers, and men, also a large hall to be used for councils and meetings; and to this he now led the captain and his officers. When they were seated, he made a speech of welcome, saying what gladness it was to him to see there those who had been so kind to him. Had he known when they would arrive, food would have been ready for them; and he assured them that, however long they might stay, they would be most heartily welcome, and that there should be no lack of provisions. They had done an immense service to him, and to all the other chiefs on the river, by breaking up the power of one who preyed upon all his neighbors, and was a scourge to trade. As there were still several bottles of the rajah's wine left, champagne was now handed round.

"It makes my heart glad to see you, Doctor," the chief said. "See, I am as strong and as well as ever. Had it not been for you, my arm might now have been useless, and my ribs have grown through the flesh."

"I don't think it would have been as bad as that," the doctor replied: "but there is no doubt that it was fortunate that you were able to receive surgical treatment so soon after the accident. And it has been fortunate for us, too, especially for our young friends here."

Conversation became general now, and the interpreter was kept hard at work, and Bahi divided her attention between the officers and the men, flitting in and out of the hall, and chattering away to the sailors and marines who were breakfasting outside on the stores they had brought up, supplemented by a bountiful supply of fruit, which grew in abundance round the village. It was not long before a meal was served to the officers, fowl having been hastily killed as soon as the boats were seen approaching; several jungle fowl had been brought in that morning; plaintains and rice were boiled, and cakes baked. Tea was forthcoming from the boats' stores, and a hearty meal was eaten.

CHAPTER XI

After the meal was concluded, the captain said to the chief:

"Now, Hassan, we want to know how it was that you arrived at the nick of time to save my officers' lives."

"I had been watching for some days," the chief said quietly. "When I heard that many chiefs had joined Sehi Pandash, I said 'I must go and help my white brothers,' but I dared not take many men away from here, and as I had to hide, the fewer there were with me the better; so I came down into the forest near Sehi's town, and found the wood full of men. We had come down in sampans, so that I could send off messengers as might be required. One of these I sent down to you, to warn you to be prepared for an attack. Other messengers I had sent before from here; but they must have been caught and killed, for I had been watched closely when they found that I would not join against you.

"When my last messenger returned, I was glad; I knew that you would be on your guard, and would not be caught treacherously. Two of my men were in the town when they began to fire on the ship, and I saw the town destroyed, and followed Sehi to the place where the six prahus were lying, and crossed the creek, and lay down in the woods near the village on the other side; for I thought that something might happen. One of my men went down in the night, and brought me news that the ship was gone. As my messenger had told me that you had questioned him as to the other entrance to the creek, I felt sure that you had gone there; so I was not surprised when, just before daybreak, two guns were fired. We saw the fight, the sinking of two of their vessels, and the attack by the water pirates, and by the men of the rajah and the chiefs with him, and I feared greatly that my friends would be overpowered.

"I sent one of my men down to the mouth of the creek, to tell you how much aid was wanted; but he saw the ship steaming up as he went, and so came back to me. Then we heard the ship's great guns begin to fire, and soon all was quiet where the fight had been going on. Then I saw the other four boats start. One of them sank before she was out of sight, and I soon heard that your ship had sunk another, and that two had got away. It was not for another two days that I learned where they were, and then I heard that they had gone into a creek twenty miles away; there one had sunk, and the other had been joined by the two prahus that had been far up the river; and I also learned that one of Sehi's men had gone into the village and let himself be captured, so that he might guide the ship's boats to the place where, as they thought, they would find but one prahu, while three would be waiting for them. I was not sure where the exact place was, for there are many creeks, but, with one of my men, I rowed in a sampan all night, in hopes to arrive in time to warn the boats; but it was not till I heard the firing that I knew exactly where they were.

"When I got there the fighting was over, and but one prahu had escaped, and I learned from the men who had swum ashore from those that had been sunk that one of the English boats had been destroyed, and many men killed, but that two boats had gone down the creek again. It was also said that the white officers and sailors had boarded the boat that had escaped, and had been all killed. I thought it best to follow the prahu, so that I could send word to you where she was to be found. As there were many passages, it was difficult to find her, and I should have lost her altogether had I not heard where Sehi was hiding, and guessed that she would go there. It was late when I arrived at the village. There one of my men learned that two young officers, who had been wounded, had been brought there, and that Sehi was sending word to you that, unless you gave him the conditions he asked, they would be put to death.

"I did not know whether to send down to you, or to send up the river for help; but I thought the last was best, for if you came in boats, then Sehi's men would hear you, and the officers would be killed; so I sent off my man with the sampan. I told him that he must not stop until he got here. He must tell them that all my men, except fifty old ones who were to guard the village, were to start in their canoes, and paddle their hardest till they came within half a mile of the village, and he was to come back with them to guide them, and I was to meet them. As the prahus that had been up there were destroyed, the river was safe for them to descend. I said that they must be at the point I named last evening. They were two hours late, though they had paddled their hardest. As soon as they disembarked I led them to the spot, and the rest was easy. I knew that the prisoners who had been taken were my two friends, for I saw them on the deck of the prahu; and glad indeed I was to be able to pay my debt to them."

"You have paid it indeed most nobly, Hassan," the captain said, holding out his hand, and grasping that of the chief, when, sentence by sentence, the story was translated to him. "Little did we think, when you were brought on board the Serpent, that your friendship would turn out of such value to us."

There was now some discussion as to the proposed meeting of chiefs; and half an hour after, a dozen small canoes started with invitations to the various chiefs to meet the captain at Hassan's campong, with assurances that he was ready to overlook their share in the attack on the ship, and be on friendly terms with them, and that the safety of each who attended was guaranteed, whether he was willing to be on good terms with the English or not. Four days later, the meeting took place in the newly erected hall. Ten or twelve of the chiefs attended; others, who had taken a leading part as Sehi's allies, did not venture to come themselves, but sent messages with assurances of their desire to be on friendly terms. A good deal of ceremonial was observed. The marines and bluejackets were drawn up in line before the hall, which was decorated with green boughs; a Union jack waved from a pole in front of it.

The chiefs were introduced by Hassan to the captain. The former then addressed them, rehearsing the service that the English had done to them by destroying the power of the tyrant who had long been a scourge to his neighbors, and who intended, without doubt, to become master of the whole district. As a proof of the good will of the English towards the Malays, he related how the two English officers had leaped into the water to save his child, and how kindly he himself had been treated. Then the captain addressed them through the interpreter. He told them that he had only been sent up the river by the Governor in accordance with an invitation from Sehi, of whose conduct he was ignorant, to undertake the protectorate of his district; and that, on learning his true character, he at once reported to the Governor that the rajah was not a proper person to receive protection, as not only did he prevent trade and harass his neighbors, but was the owner of a number of piratical craft, that often descended the river and plundered the coast.

"England," he went on, "has no desire whatever to take under her protection any who do not earnestly desire it, and who are not willing, in return, to promote trade, and keep peace with their neighbors; nor can she make separate arrangements with minor chiefs. It was only because she understood that Sehi ruled over a considerable extent of territory, and was all powerful in this part, that his request was listened to.

"I shall shortly return down the river," he said, "and have no thought or intention of interfering in any way with matters here. I wish to leave on good terms with you all, and to explain to you that it is to your interest to do all in your power to further trade, both by sending down your products to the coast, and by throwing no hindrance in the way of the products of the highlands coming down the river, charging, at the utmost, a very small toll upon each boat that passes up and down. It is the interest of all of you, of the people of the hills, and of ourselves, that trade should increase. Now that Sehi is dead and his people altogether dispersed and all his piratical craft destroyed, with the exception of the one captured by Hassan, there is no obstruction to trade, and you are free from the fear that he would one day eat you up.

"Be assured that there is nothing to be feared from us. You all know how greatly the States protected by us have flourished and how wealthy their rajahs have become from the increase of cultivation and the cessation of tribal wars. If in the future all the chiefs of this district should desire to place themselves under English protection, their request will be considered; but there is not the slightest desire on the part of the Governor to assume further responsibility, and he will be well satisfied indeed to know that there is peace among the river tribes, security for trade, and a large increase in the cultivation of the country and in its prosperity."

There was a general expression of satisfaction and relief upon the face of the chiefs, as, sentence by sentence, the speech was translated to them; and, one by one, they rose after its conclusion, and expressed their hearty concurrence with what had been said.

"We know," one of them said, "that these wars do much harm; but if we quarrel, or if one ill treats another, or encourages his slaves to leave him, or ravages his plantations, what are we to do?"

"That I have thought of," the captain said. "I have spoken with the chief Hassan, and he has agreed to remove with his people to the spot where Sehi's town stood. There, doubtless, he will be joined by Sehi's former subjects, who cannot but be well pleased at being rid of a tyrant who had forcibly taken them under his rule. He will retain the prahu that he has taken, and will use it to keep the two rivers free of robbers, but in no other respect will he interfere with his neighbors. His desire is to cultivate the land, clear away the forest, and encourage his people to raise products that he can send down the river to trade with us. He will occupy the territory only as far as the creek that runs between the two rivers. I propose that all of you shall come to an agreement to submit any disputes that may arise between you to his decision, swearing to accept his judgment, whichever way it may go. This is the way in which the disputes are settled in our country. Both sides go before a judge, and he hears their statements and those of their witnesses, and then decides the case; and even the government of the country is bound by his decision. I don't wish you to give me any reply as to this. I make the suggestion solely for your own good, and it is for you to talk it over among yourselves, and see if you cannot all come to an agreement that will put a stop to the senseless wars, and enable your people to cultivate the land in peace, and to obtain all the comforts that arise from trade."

A boat had been sent down to the ship, and this returned with a number of the articles that had been put on board her as presents for Sehi and other chiefs. These were now distributed. A feast was then held, and the next morning the chiefs started for their homes, highly gratified with the result of the meeting. On the following day, the British boats also took their way down the river, followed by the prahu, with a considerable number of Hassan's men, who were to clear away the ruins of Sehi's campong, to bury the dead still lying among them, and to erect huts for the whole community. The Serpent remained for a week opposite the town; a considerable quantity of flour, sugar, and other useful stores being landed for the use of Hassan's people. Dr. Horsley was gladdened by Hassan's promise that his people should be instructed to search for specimens of birds, butterflies, and other insects, and that these should be treated according to his instructions, and should be from time to time, as occasion offered, sent down to him in large cases to Singapore. To the two midshipmen the chief gave krises of the finest temper.

"I have no presents to give you worthy of your acceptance," he said; "but you know that I shall never forget you, and always regard you as brothers. I intend to send twelve of my young men down to Penang, there to live for three years and learn useful trades from your people. The doctor has advised me also to send Bahi, and has promised to find a comfortable home for her, where she will learn to read and write your language and many other useful things. It is hard to part with her; but it is for her good and that of her people. If you will write to me sometimes, she will read the letters to me and write letters to you in return, so that, though we are away from each other, we may know that neither of us has forgotten the other."

Bahi and twelve young Malays were taken to Penang in the Serpent, where the doctor found a comfortable home for her with some friends of his, to whom payment for her board and schooling was to be paid by Hassan in blocks of tin, which he would obtain from boats coming down from the hills in exchange for other articles of trade. The Malays were placed with men of their own race belonging to the protected States, and settled as carpenters, smiths, and other tradesmen in Penang. Three years later, they and Bahi were all taken back in the Serpent to their home.

The river was acquiring considerable importance from the great increase of trade. They found Hassan's town far more extensive and flourishing than it had been in the time of its predecessor. The forest had been cleared for a considerable distance round it, the former inhabitants had returned, tobacco, sugar canes, cotton, pepper, and other crops whose products were useful for trade purposes, were largely cultivated, while orchards of fruit trees had been extensively planted. Hassan reported that tribal wars had almost ceased, and that disputes were in almost all cases brought for his arbitration. Owing to the abolition of all oppressive tolls, trade from the interior had very largely increased, a great deal of tin, together with spices and other products, now finding its way down by the river. Hassan was delighted with the progress Bahi had made, and ordered that three or four boys should at once be placed for instruction under each of the men who had learned trades at Penang.

There was much regret on both sides when the Serpent again started down the river; for it was known that she would not return, as in a few months she would be sent to a Chinese station, and from there would go direct to England. The composition of her crew was already somewhat changed. Lieutenant Ferguson had received his promotion for the fight with the prahus, and had been appointed to the command of a gunboat whose captain had been invalided home. Lieutenant Hopkins was now the Serpent's first lieutenant, and Morrison was second. Harry Parkhurst was third lieutenant, Dick Balderson, to the regret of both, having left the ship on his promotion, and having been transferred as third lieutenant to Captain Ferguson's craft. Both have since kept up a correspondence with Bahi, who has married a neighboring chief, and who tells them that the river is prospering greatly, and that, although he assumes no authority, her father is everywhere regarded as the paramount chief of the district. From time to time each receives chests filled with spices, silks, and other Malay products, and sends back in return European articles of utility to the rajah, for such is the rank that Hassan has now acquired on the river.

G. A. Henty

Bears And Dacoits A Tale Of The Ghauts

CHAPTER I

A merry party were sitting in the veranda of one of the largest and handsomest bungalows of Poonah. It belonged to Colonel Hastings, colonel of a native regiment stationed there, and at present, in virtue of seniority, commanding a brigade. Tiffin was on, and three or four officers and four ladies had taken their seats in the comfortable cane lounging chairs which form the invariable furniture of the veranda of a well ordered bungalow. Permission had been duly asked, and granted by Mrs. Hastings, and the cheroots had just begun to draw, when Miss Hastings, a niece of the colonel, who had only arrived the previous week from England, said: "Uncle, I am quite disappointed. Mrs. Lyons showed me the bear she has got tied up in their compound, and it is the most wretched little thing, not bigger than Rover, papa's retriever, and it's full grown. I thought bears were great fierce creatures, and this poor little thing seemed so restless and unhappy that I thought it quite a shame not to let it go."

Colonel Hastings smiled rather grimly.

"And yet, small and insignificant as that bear is, my dear, it is a question whether he is not as dangerous an animal to meddle with as a man eating tiger."

"What, that wretched little bear, uncle?"

"Yes, that wretched little bear. Any experienced sportsman will tell you that hunting those little bears is as dangerous a sport as tiger hunting on foot, to say nothing of tiger hunting from an elephant's back, in which there is scarcely any danger whatever. I can speak feelingly about it, for my career was pretty nearly brought to an end by a bear, just after I entered the army, some thirty years ago, at a spot within a few miles from here. I have got the scars on my shoulder and arm still."

"Oh, do tell me all about it," Miss Hastings said; and the request being seconded by the rest of the party, none of whom, with the exception of Mrs. Hastings, had ever heard the story before—for the colonel was somewhat chary of relating this special experience—he waited till they had all drawn up their chairs as close as possible, and then giving two or three vigorous puffs at his cheroot, began as follows:

"Thirty years ago, in 1855, things were not so settled in the Deccan as they are now. There was no idea of insurrection on a large scale, but we were going through one of those outbreaks of Dacoity which have several times proved so troublesome. Bands of marauders kept the country in confusion, pouring down on a village, now carrying off three or four of the Bombay money lenders, who were then, as now, the curse of the country; sometimes making an onslaught upon a body of traders; and occasionally venturing to attack small detachments of troops or isolated parties of police. They were not very formidable, but they were very troublesome, and most difficult to catch, for the peasantry regarded them as patriots, and aided and shielded them in every way. The headquarters of these gangs of Dacoits were the Ghauts. In the thick bush and deep valleys and gorges there they could always take refuge, while sometimes the more daring chiefs converted these detached peaks and masses of rock, numbers of which you can see as you come up the Ghaut by railway, into almost impregnable fortresses. Many of these masses of rock rise as sheer up from the hillside as walls of masonry, and look at a short distance like ruined castles. Some are absolutely inaccessible; others can only be scaled by experienced climbers; and, although possible for the natives with their bare feet, are impracticable to European troops. Many of these rock fortresses were at various times the headquarters of famous Dacoit leaders, and unless the summits happened to be commanded from some higher ground within gunshot range they were all but impregnable, except by starvation. When driven to bay, these fellows would fight well.

"Well, about the time I joined, the Dacoits were unusually troublesome; the police had a hard time of it, and almost lived in the saddle, and the cavalry were constantly called up to help them, while detachments of infantry from the station were under canvas at several places along the top of the Ghauts to cut the bands off from their strongholds, and to aid, if necessary, in turning them out of their rock fortresses. The natives in the valleys at the foot of the Ghauts, who have always been a semi-independent race, ready to rob whenever they saw a chance, were great friends with the Dacoits and supplied them with provisions whenever the hunt on the Deccan was too hot to make raids in that direction.

"This is a long introduction, you will say, and does not seem to have much to do with bears; but it is really necessary, as you will see. I had joined about six months when three companies of the regiment were ordered to relieve a wing of the 15th, who had been under canvas at a village some four miles to the north of the point where the line crosses the top of the Ghauts. There were three white officers, and little enough to do, except when a party was sent off to assist the police. We had one or two brushes with the Dacoits, but I was not out on either occasion. However, there was plenty of shooting, and a good many pigs about, so we had very good fun. Of course, as a raw hand, I was very hot for it, and as the others had both passed the enthusiastic age, except for pig sticking and big game, I could always get away. I was supposed not to go far from camp, because in the first place, I might be wanted; and, in the second, because of the Dacoits; and Norworthy, who was in command, used to impress upon me that I ought not to go beyond the sound of a bugle. Of course we both knew that if I intended to get any sport I must go further afoot than this; but I merely used to say 'All right, sir, I will keep an ear to the camp,' and he on his part never considered it necessary to ask where the game which appeared on the table came from. But in point of fact, I never went very far, and my servant always had instructions which way to send for me if I was wanted; while, as to the Dacoits, I did not believe in their having the impudence to come in broad daylight within a mile or two of our camp. I did not often go down the face of the Ghauts. The shooting was good, and there were plenty of bears in those days, but it needed a long day for such an expedition, and in view of the Dacoits who might be scattered about, was not the sort of thing to be undertaken except with a strong party. Norworthy had not given any precise orders about it, but I must admit that he said one day:

"'Of course you won't be fool enough to think of going down the Ghauts, Hastings?' But I did not look at that as equivalent to a direct order—whatever I should do now," the colonel put in, on seeing a furtive smile on the faces of his male listeners.

"However, I never meant to go down, though I used to stand on the edge and look longingly down into the bush and fancy I saw bears moving about in scores. But I don't think I should have gone into their country if they had not come into mine. One day the fellow who always carried my spare gun or flask, and who was a sort of shikaree in a small way, told me he had heard that a farmer whose house stood near the edge of the Ghauts, some two miles away, had been seriously annoyed by his fruit and corn being stolen by bears.

"'I'll go and have a look at the place tomorrow,' I said; 'there is no parade, and I can start early. You may as well tell the mess cook to put up a basket with some tiffin and a bottle of claret, and get a boy to carry it over.'

"'The bears not come in day,' Rahman said.

"'Of course not,' I replied; 'still I may like to find out which way they come. Just do as you are told.'

"The next morning, at seven o'clock, I was at the farmer's spoken of, and there was no mistake as to the bears. A patch of Indian corn had been ruined by them, and two dogs had been killed. The native was in a terrible state of rage and alarm. He said that on moonlight nights he had seen eight of them, and they came and sniffed around the door of the cottage.

"'Why don't you fire through the window at them?' I asked scornfully, for I had seen a score of tame bears in captivity, and, like you, Mary, was inclined to despise them, though there was far less excuse for me; for I had heard stories which should have convinced me that, small as he is, the Indian bear is not a beast to be attacked with impunity. Upon walking to the edge of the Ghauts there was no difficulty in discovering the route by which the bears came up to the farm. For a mile to the right and left the ground fell away as if cut with a knife, leaving a precipice of over a hundred feet sheer down; but close by where I was standing was the head of a water course, which in time had gradually worn a sort of cleft in the wall, up or down which it was not difficult to make one's way. Further down this little gorge widened out and became a deep ravine, and further still a wide valley, where it opened upon the flats far below us. About half a mile down, where the ravine was deepest and darkest, was a thick clump of trees and jungle.

"'That's where the bears are?' I asked Rahman. He nodded. It seemed no distance. I could get down and back in time for tiffin, and perhaps bag a couple of bears. For a young sportsman the temptation was great. 'How long would it take us to go down and have a shot or two at them?'

"'No good go down. Master come here at night, shoot bears when they come up.'

"I had thought of that; but, in the first place, it did not seem much sport to shoot the beasts from cover when they were quietly eating, and, in the next place, I knew that Norworthy could not, even if he were willing, give me leave to go out of camp at night. I waited, hesitating for a few minutes, and then I said to myself, 'It is of no use waiting. I could go down and get a bear and be back again while I am thinking of it;' then to Rahman, 'No, come along; we will have a look through that wood anyhow.'

"Rahman evidently did not like it. 'Not easy to find bear, sahib. He very cunning.'

"'Well, very likely we shan't find them,' I said, 'but we can try anyhow. Bring that bottle with you; the tiffin basket can wait here till we come back.' In another five minutes I had begun to climb down the watercourse—the shikaree following me. I took the double barreled rifle and handed him the shotgun, having first dropped a bullet down each barrel over the charge. The ravine was steep, but there were bushes to hold on by, and although it was hot work and took a good deal longer than I expected, we at last got down to the place which I had fixed upon as likely to be the bears' home.

"'Sahib, climb up top,' Rahman said; 'come down through wood; no good fire at bear when he above.'

"I had heard that before; but I was hot, the sun was pouring down, there was not a breath of wind, and it looked a long way up to the top of the wood.

"'Give me the claret. It would take too long to search the wood regularly. We will sit down here for a bit, and if we can see anything moving up in the wood, well and good; if not, we will come back again another day with some beaters and dogs.' So saying, I sat down with my back against a rock, at a spot where I could look up among the trees for a long way through a natural vista. I had a drink of claret, and then I sat and watched till gradually I dropped off to sleep. I don't know how long I slept, but it was some time, and I woke up with a sudden start. Rahman, who had, I fancy, been asleep too, also started up.

"The noise which had aroused us was made by a rolling stone striking a rock: and looking up I saw some fifty yards away, not in the wood, but on the rocky hillside on our side of the ravine, a bear standing, as though unconscious of our presence, snuffing the air. As was natural, I seized my rifle, cocked it, and took aim, unheeding a cry of 'No, no, sahib,' from Rahman. However, I was not going to miss such a chance as this, and I let fly. The beast had been standing sideways to me, and as I saw him fall I felt sure I had hit him in the heart. I gave a shout of triumph, and was about to climb up, when, from behind the rock on which the bear had stood, appeared another, growling fiercely; on seeing me, it at once prepared to come down. Stupidly, being taken by surprise, and being new at it, I fired at once at its head. The bear gave a spring, and then—it seemed instantaneous—down it came at me. Whether it rolled down, or slipped down, or ran down, I don't know, but it came almost as if it had jumped straight at me.

"'My gun, Rahman,' I shouted, holding out my hand. There was no answer. I glanced round and found that the scoundrel had bolted. I had time, and only just time, to take a step backwards, and to club my rifle, when the brute was upon me. I got one fair blow at the side of its head, a blow that would have smashed the skull of any civilized beast into pieces, and which did fortunately break the brute's jaw; then in an instant he was upon me, and I was fighting for life. My hunting knife was out, and with my left hand I had the beast by the throat; while with my right I tried to drive my knife into its ribs. My bullet had gone through his chest. The impetus of his charge had knocked me over, and we rolled on the ground, he tearing with his claws at my shoulder and arm, I stabbing and struggling; my great effort being to keep my knees up so as to protect my body with them from his hind claws. After the first blow with his paw which laid my shoulder open, I do not think I felt any special pain whatever. There was a strange faint sensation, and my whole energy seemed centered in the two ideas—to strike and to keep my knees up. I knew that I was getting faint, but I was dimly conscious that his efforts, too, were relaxing. His weight on me seemed to increase enormously, and the last idea that flashed across me was that it was a drawn fight.

"The next idea of which I was conscious was that I was being carried. I seemed to be swinging about, and I thought I was at sea. Then there was a little jolt and a sense of pain. 'A collision,' I muttered, and opened my eyes. Beyond the fact that I seemed in a yellow world—a bright orange yellow—my eyes did not help me, and I lay vaguely wondering about it all, till the rocking ceased. There was another bump, and then the yellow world seemed to come to an end; and as the daylight streamed in upon me I fainted again. This time, when I awoke to consciousness, things were clearer. I was stretched by a little stream. A native woman was sprinkling my face and washing the blood from my wounds; while another, who had with my own knife cut off my coat and shirt, was tearing the latter into strips to bandage my wounds. The yellow world was explained. I was lying on the yellow robe of one of the women. They had tied the ends together, placed a long stick through them, and carried me in the bag-like hammock. They nodded to me when they saw I was conscious, and brought water in a large leaf, and poured it into my mouth. Then one went away for some time, and came back with some leaves and bark. These they chewed and put on my wounds, bound them up with strips of my shirt, and then again knotted the ends of the cloth, and lifting me up, went on as before.

"I was sure that we were much lower down the Ghaut than we had been when I was watching for the bears, and we were now going still lower. However, I knew very little Hindustani, nothing of the language the women spoke. I was too weak to stand, too weak even to think much; and I dozed and woke, and dozed again until, after what seemed to me many hours of travel, we stopped again, this time before a tent. Two or three old women and four or five men came out, and there was great talking between them and the young women—for they were young—who had carried me down. Some of the party appeared angry; but at last things quieted down, and I was carried into the tent. I had fever, and was, I suppose, delirious for days. I afterwards found that for fully a fortnight I had lost all consciousness; but a good constitution and the nursing of the women pulled me round. When once the fever had gone, I began to mend rapidly. I tried to explain to the women that if they would go up to the camp and tell them where I was they would be well rewarded; but although I was sure they understood, they shook their heads, and by the fact that as I became stronger two or three armed men always hung about the tent, I came to the conclusion that I was a sort of prisoner. This was annoying, but did not seem serious. If these people were Dacoits, or, as was more likely, allies of the Dacoits, I could be kept only for ransom or exchange. Moreover, I felt sure of my ability to escape when I got strong, especially as I believed that in the young women who had saved my life, both by bringing me down and by their careful nursing, I should find friends."

"Were they pretty, uncle?" Mary Hastings broke in.

"Never mind whether they were pretty, Mary; they were better than pretty."

"No; but we should like to know, uncle."

"Well, except for the soft, dark eyes, common to the race, and the good temper and lightheartedness, also so general among Hindu girls, and the tenderness which women feel towards a creature whose life they have saved, whether it is a wounded bird or a drowning puppy, I suppose they were nothing remarkable in the way of beauty, but at the time I know that I thought them charming."

CHAPTER II

"Just as I was getting strong enough to walk, and was beginning to think of making my escape, a band of five or six fellows, armed to the teeth, came in, and made signs that I was to go with them. It was evidently an arranged thing, the girls only were surprised, but they were at once turned out, and as we started I could see two crouching figures in the shade with their cloths over their heads. I had a native garment thrown over my shoulders, and in five minutes after the arrival of the fellows found myself on my way. It took us some six hours before we reached our destination, which was one of those natural rock citadels. Had I been in my usual health I could have done the distance in an hour and a half, but I had to rest constantly, and was finally carried rather than helped up. I had gone not unwillingly, for the men were clearly, by their dress, Dacoits of the Deccan, and I had no doubt that it was intended either to ransom or exchange me.

"At the foot of this natural castle were some twenty or thirty more robbers, and I was led to a rough sort of arbor in which was lying, on a pile of maize straw, a man who was evidently their chief. He rose and we exchanged salaams.

"'What is your name, sahib?' he asked in Mahratta.

"'Hastings—Lieutenant Hastings,' I said. 'And yours?'

"'Sivajee Punt!' he said.

"This was bad. I had fallen into the hands of the most troublesome, most ruthless, and most famous of the Dacoit leaders. Over and over again he had been hotly chased, but had always managed to get away; and when I last heard anything of what was going on four or five troops of native police were scouring the country after him. He gave an order which I did not understand, and a wretched Bombay writer, I suppose a clerk of some moneylender, was dragged forward. Sivajee Punt spoke to him for some time, and the fellow then told me in English that I was to write at once to the officer commanding the troops, telling him that I was in his hands, and should be put to death directly he was attacked.

"'Ask him,' I said, 'if he will take any sum of money to let me go?'

"Sivajee shook his head very decidedly.

"A piece of paper was put before me, and a pen and ink, and I wrote as I had been ordered, adding however, in French, that I had brought myself into my present position by my own folly, and would take my chance, for I well knew the importance which government attached to Sivajee's capture. I read out loud all that I had written in English, and the interpreter translated it. Then the paper was folded and I addressed it, 'The Officer Commanding,' and I was given some chupattis and a drink of water, and allowed to sleep. The Dacoits had apparently no fear of any immediate attack.

"It was still dark, although morning was just breaking, when I was awakened, and was got up to the citadel. I was hoisted rather than climbed, two men standing above with a rope, tied round my body, so that I was half hauled, half pushed up the difficult places, which would have taxed all my climbing powers had I been in health.

Among Malay Pirates

"The height of this mass of rock was about a hundred feet; the top was fairly flat, with some depressions and risings, and about eighty feet long by fifty wide. It had evidently been used as a fortress in ages past. Along the side facing the hill were the remains of a rough wall. In the center of a depression was a cistern, some four feet square, lined with stone work, and in another depression a gallery had been cut, leading to a subterranean storeroom or chamber.

"This natural fortress rose from the face of the hill at a distance of a thousand yards or so from the edge of the plateau, which was fully two hundred feet higher than the top of the rock. In the old days it would have been impregnable, and even at that time it was an awkward place to take, for the troops were armed only with Brown Bess, and rifled cannon were not thought of. Looking round, I could see that I was some four miles from the point where I had descended. The camp was gone; but running my eye along the edge of the plateau I could see the tops of tents a mile to my right, and again two miles to my left; turning round, and looking down into the wide valley, I saw a regimental camp.

"It was evident that a vigorous effort was being made to surround and capture the Dacoits, since troops had been brought up from Bombay. In addition to the troops above and below, there would probably be a strong police force, acting on the face of the hill. I did not see all these things at the time, for I was, as soon as I got to the top, ordered to sit down behind the parapet, a fellow armed to the teeth squatting down by me, and signifying that if I showed my head above the stones he would cut my throat without hesitation. There were, however, sufficient gaps between the stones to allow me to have a view of the crest of the Ghaut, while below my view extended down to the hills behind Bombay. It was evident to me now why the Dacoits did not climb up into the fortress. There were dozens of similar crags on the face of the Ghauts, and the troops did not as yet know their whereabouts. It was a sort of blockade of the whole face of the hills which was being kept up, and there were, probably enough, several other bands of Dacoits lurking in the jungle.

"There were only two guards and myself on the rock plateau. I discussed with myself the chances of my overpowering them and holding the top of the rock till help came; but I was greatly weakened, and was not a match for a boy, much less for the two stalwart Mahrattas; besides, I was by no means sure that the way I had been brought up was the only possible path to the top. The day passed off quietly. The heat on the bare rock was frightful, but one of the men, seeing how weak and ill I really was, fetched a thick rug from the storehouse, and with the aid of a stick made a sort of lean-to against the wall, under which I lay sheltered from the sun.

"Once or twice during the day I heard a few distant musket shots, and once a sharp, heavy outburst of firing. It must have been three or four miles away, but it was on the side of the Ghaut, and showed that the troops or police were at work. My guards looked anxiously in that direction, and uttered sundry curses. When it was dusk, Sivajee and eight of the Dacoits came up. From what they said, I gathered that the rest of the band had dispersed, trusting either to get through the line of their pursuers, or, if caught, to escape with slight punishment, the men who remained being too deeply concerned in murderous outrages to hope for mercy. Sivajee himself handed me a letter, which the man who had taken my note had brought back in reply. Major Knapp, the writer, who was the second in command, said that he could not engage the Government, but that if Lieutenant Hastings was given up the act would certainly dispose the Government to take the most merciful view possible; but that if, on the contrary, any harm was suffered by Lieutenant Hastings, every man taken would be at once hung. Sivajee did not appear put out about it. I do not think he expected any other answer, and imagine that his real object in writing was simply to let them know that I was a prisoner, and so enable him the better to paralyze the attack upon a position which he no doubt considered all but impregnable.

"I was given food, and was then allowed to walk as I chose upon the little plateau, two of the Dacoits taking post as sentries at the steepest part of the path, while the rest gathered, chatting and smoking, in the depression in front of the storehouse. It was still light enough for me to see for some distance down the face of the rock, and I strained my eyes to see if I could discern any other spot at which an ascent or descent was possible. The prospect was not encouraging. At some places the face fell sheer away from the edge, and so evident was the impracticability of escape that the only place which I glanced at twice was the western side, that is the one away from the hill. Here it sloped gradually for a few feet. I took off my shoes and went down to the edge. Below, some ten feet, was a ledge, on to which with care I could get down, but below that was a sheer fall of some fifty feet. As a means of escape it was hopeless, but it struck me that if an attack was made I might slip away and get on to the ledge. Once there I could not be seen except by a person standing where I now was, just on the edge of the slope, a spot to which it was very unlikely that anyone would come.

"The thought gave me a shadow of hope, and, returning to the upper end of the platform, I lay down, and in spite of the hardness of the rock, was soon asleep. The pain of my aching bones woke me up several times, and once, just as the first tinge of dawn was coming, I thought I could hear movements in the jungle. I raised myself somewhat, and I saw that the sounds had been heard by the Dacoits, for they were standing listening, and some of them were bringing spare firearms from the storehouse, in evident preparation for attack.

"As I afterwards learned, the police had caught one of the Dacoits trying to effect his escape, and by means of a little of the ingenious torture to which the Indian police then frequently resorted, when their white officers were absent, they obtained from him the exact position of Sivajee's band, and learned the side from which the ascent must be made. That the Dacoit and his band were still upon the slopes of the Ghauts they knew, and were gradually narrowing their circle, but there were so many rocks and hiding places that the process of searching was a slow one, and the intelligence was so important that the news was off at once to the colonel, who gave orders for the police to surround the rock at daylight and to storm it if possible. The garrison was so small that the police were alone ample for the work, supposing that the natural difficulties were not altogether insuperable.

"Just at daybreak there was a distant noise of men moving in the jungle, and the Dacoit halfway down the path fired his gun. He was answered by a shout and a volley. The Dacoits hurried out from the chamber, and lay down on the edge, where, sheltered by a parapet, they commanded the path. They paid no attention to me, and I kept as far away as possible. The fire began—a quiet, steady fire, a shot at a time and in strong contrast to the rattle kept up from the surrounding jungle; but every shot must have told, as man after man who strove to climb that steep path fell. It lasted only ten minutes, and then all was quiet again.

"The attack had failed, as I knew it must do, for two men could have held the place against an army; a quarter of an hour later a gun from the crest above spoke out, and a round shot whistled above our heads. Beyond annoyance, an artillery fire could do no harm, for the party could be absolutely safe in the store cave. The instant the shot flew overhead, however, Sivajee Punt beckoned to me, and motioned me to take my seat on the wall facing the guns. Hesitation was useless, and I took my seat with my back to the Dacoits and my face to the hill. One of the Dacoits, as I did so, pulled off the native cloth which covered my shoulders, in order that I might be clearly seen.

"Just as I took my place another round shot hummed by; but then there was a long interval of silence. With a field glass every feature must have been distinguishable to the gunners, and I had no doubt that they were waiting for orders as to what to do next.

"I glanced round and saw that, with the exception of one fellow squatted behind the parapet some half dozen yards away, clearly as a sentry to keep me in place, all the others had disappeared. Some, no doubt, were on sentry down the path, the others were in the store beneath me. After half an hour's silence the guns spoke out again. Evidently the gunners were told to be as careful as they could, for some of the shots went wide on the left, others on the right. A few struck the rock below me. The situation was not pleasant, but I thought that at a thousand yards they ought not to hit me, and I tried to distract my attention by thinking out what I should do under every possible contingency.

"Presently I felt a crash and a shock, and fell backwards to the ground. I was not hurt, and picking myself up saw that the ball had struck the parapet to the left, just where my guard was sitting, and he lay covered with its fragments. His turban lay some yards behind him. Whether he was dead or not I neither knew nor cared.

"I pushed down some of the parapet where I had been sitting, dropped my cap on the edge outside, so as to make it appear that I had fallen over, and then, picking up the man's turban, ran to the other end of the platform and scrambled down to the ledge. Then I began to wave my arms about—I had nothing on above the waist—and in a moment I saw a face with a uniform cap peer out through the jungle; and a hand was waved. I made signs to him to make his way to the foot of the perpendicular wall of rock beneath me. I then unwound the turban, whose length was, I knew, amply sufficient to reach to the bottom, and then looked round for something to write on. I had my pencil still in my trousers pocket, but not a scrap of paper.

"I picked up a flattish piece of rock and wrote on it, 'Get a rope ladder quickly, I can haul it up. Ten men in garrison. They are all under cover. Keep on firing to distract their attention.'

"I tied the stone to the end of the turban, and looked over. A noncommissioned officer of the police was already standing below. I lowered the stone; he took it, waved his hand to me, and was gone.

"An hour passed: it seemed an age. The round shots still rang overhead, and the fire was now much more heavy and sustained than before. Presently I again saw a movement in the jungle, and Norworthy's face appeared, and he waved his arm in greeting.

"Five minutes more and a party were gathered at the foot of the rock, and a strong rope was tied to the cloth. I pulled it up. A rope ladder was attached to it, and the top rung was in a minute or two in my hands. To it was tied a piece of paper with the words: 'Can you fasten the ladder?' I wrote on the paper: 'No; but I can hold it for a light weight.'

"I put the paper with a stone in the end of the cloth, and lowered it again. Then I sat down, tied the rope round my waist, got my feet against two projections, and waited. There was a jerk, and then I felt someone was coming up the rope ladder. The strain was far less than I expected, but the native policeman who came up first did not weigh half so much as an average Englishman. There were now two of us to hold. The officer in command of the police came up next, then Norworthy, then a dozen more police. I explained the situation, and we mounted to the upper level. Not a soul was to be seen. Quickly we advanced and took up a position to command the door of the underground chamber; while one of the police waved a white cloth from his bayonet as a signal to the gunners to cease firing. Then the officer hailed the party within the cave.

"'Sivajee Punt! you may as well come out and give yourself up! We are in possession, and resistance is useless!'

"A yell of rage and surprise was heard, and the Dacoits, all desperate men, came bounding out, firing as they did so. Half of their number were shot down at once and the rest, after a short, sharp struggle, were bound hand and foot.

"That is pretty well all of the story, I think. Sivajee Punt was one of the killed. The prisoners were all either hung or imprisoned for life. I escaped my blowing up for having gone down the Ghauts after the bear, because, after all, Sivajee Punt might have defied their force for months had I not done so.

"It seemed that that scoundrel Rahman had taken back word that I was killed. Norworthy had sent down a strong party, who found the two dead bears, and who, having searched everywhere without finding any signs of my body, came to the conclusion that I had been found and carried away, especially as they ascertained that natives used that path. They had offered rewards, but nothing was heard of me till my note saying I was in Sivajee's hands arrived."

"And did you ever see the women who carried you off?"

"No, Mary, I never saw them again. I did, however, after immense trouble, succeed in finding out where it was that I had been taken to. I went down at once, but found the village deserted. Then after much inquiry I found where the people had moved to, and sent messages to the women to come up to the camp, but they never came; and I was reduced at last to sending them down two sets of silver bracelets, necklaces, and bangles, which must have rendered them the envy of all the women on the Ghauts. They sent back a message of grateful thanks, and I never heard of them afterwards. No doubt their relatives, who knew that their connection with the Dacoits was now known, would not let them come. However, I had done all I could and I have no doubt the women were perfectly satisfied. So you see, my dear, that the Indian bear, small as he is, is an animal which it is as well to leave alone, at any rate when he happens to be up on the side of a hill while you are at the foot."

The Paternosters

"And do you really mean that we are to cross by the steamer, Mr. Virtue, while you go over in the Seabird? I do not approve of that at all. Fanny, why do you not rebel, and say we won't be put ashore? I call it horrid, after a fortnight on board this dear little yacht, to have to get on to a crowded steamer, with no accommodation and lots of seasick women, perhaps, and crying children. You surely cannot be in earnest?"

"I do not like it any more than you do, Minnie; but, as Tom says we had better do it, and my husband agrees with him, I am afraid we must submit. Do you really think it is quite necessary, Mr. Virtue? Minnie and I are both good sailors, you know; and we would much rather have a little extra tossing about on board the Seabird than the discomforts of a steamer."

"I certainly think that it will be best, Mrs. Grantham. You know very well we would rather have you on board, and that we shall suffer from your loss more than you will by going the other way; but there's no doubt the wind is getting up, and though we don't feel it much here, it must be blowing pretty hard outside. The Seabird is as good a seaboat as anything of her size that floats; but you don't know what it is to be out in anything like a heavy sea in a thirty tonner. It would be impossible for you to stay on deck, and we should have our hands full, and should not be able to give you the benefit of our society. Personally, I should not mind being out in the Seabird in any weather, but I would certainly rather not have ladies on board."

"You don't think we should scream, or do anything foolish, Mr. Virtue?" Minnie Graham said indignantly.

"Not at all, Miss Graham. Still, I repeat, the knowledge that there are women on board, delightful at other times, does not tend to comfort in bad weather. Of course, if you prefer it, we can put off our start till this puff of wind has blown itself out. It may have dropped before morning. It may last some little time. I don't think myself that it will drop, for the glass has fallen, and I am afraid we may have a spell of broken weather."

"Oh, no; don't put it off," Mrs. Grantham said; "we have only another fortnight before James must be back again in London, and it would be a great pity to lose three or four days perhaps; and we have been looking forward to cruising about among the Channel Islands, and to St. Mao, and all those places. Oh, no; I think the other is much the better plan—that is if you won't take us with you."

"It would be bad manners to say that I won't, Mrs. Grantham; but I must say I would rather not. It will be a very short separation. Grantham will take you on shore at once, and as soon as the boat comes back I shall be off. You will start in the steamer this evening, and get into Jersey at nine or ten o'clock tomorrow morning; and if I am not there before you, I shall not be many hours after you."

"Well, if it must be it must," Mrs. Grantham said, with an air of resignation. "Come, Minnie, let us put a few things into a handbag for tonight. You see the skipper is not to be moved by our pleadings."

"That is the worst of you married women, Fanny," Miss Graham said, with a little pout. "You get into the way of doing as you are ordered. I call it too bad. Here have we been cruising about for the last fortnight, with scarcely a breath of wind, and longing for a good brisk breeze and a little change and excitement, and now it comes at last, we are to be packed off in a steamer. I call it horrid of you, Mr. Virtue. You may laugh, but I do."

Tom Virtue laughed, but he showed no signs of giving way, and ten minutes later Mr. and Mrs. Grantham and Miss Graham took their places in the gig, and were rowed into Southampton Harbor, off which the Seabird was lying.

The last fortnight had been a very pleasant one, and it had cost the owner of the Seabird as much as his guests to come to the conclusion that it was better to break up the party for a few hours.

Tom Virtue had, up to the age of five-and-twenty, been possessed of a sufficient income for his wants. He had entered at the bar, not that he felt any particular vocation in that direction, but because he thought it incumbent upon him to do something. Then, at the death of an uncle, he had come into a considerable fortune, and was able to indulge his taste for yachting, which was the sole amusement for which he really cared, to the fullest.

He sold the little five tonner he had formerly possessed, and purchased the Seabird. He could well have afforded a much larger craft, but he knew that there was far more real enjoyment in sailing to be obtained from a small craft than a large one, for in the latter he would be obliged to have a regular skipper, and would be little more than a passenger, whereas on board the Seabird, although his first hand was dignified by the name of skipper, he was himself the absolute master. The boat carried the aforesaid skipper, three hands, and a steward, and with them he had twice been up the Mediterranean, across to Norway, and had several times made the circuit of the British Isles.

He had unlimited confidence in his boat, and cared not what weather he was out in her. This was the first time since his ownership of her that the Seabird had carried lady passengers. His friend Grantham, an old school and college chum, was a hard working barrister, and Virtue had proposed to him to take a month's holiday on board the Seabird.

"Put aside your books, old man," he said. "You look fagged and overworked; a month's blow will do you all the good in the world."

"Thank you, Tom; I have made up my mind for a month's holiday, but I can't accept your invitation, though I should enjoy it of all things. But it would not be fair to my wife; she doesn't get very much of my society, and she has been looking forward to our having a run together. So I must decline."

Virtue hesitated a moment. He was not very fond of ladies' society, and thought them especially in the way on board a yacht; but he had a great liking for his friend's wife, and was almost as much at home in his house as in his own chambers.

"Why not bring the wife with you?" he said, as soon as his mind was made up. "It will be a nice change for her too; and I have heard her say that she is a good sailor. The accommodation is not extensive, but the after cabin is a pretty good size, and I would do all I could to make her comfortable. Perhaps she would like another lady with her; if so by all means bring one. They could have the after cabin, you could have the little stateroom, and I could sleep in the saloon."

"It is very good of you, Tom, especially as I know that it will put you out frightfully; but the offer is a very tempting one. I will speak to Fanny, and let you have an answer in the morning."

"That will be delightful, James," Mrs. Grantham said, when the invitation was repeated to her. "I should like it of all things; and I am sure the rest and quiet and the sea air will be just the thing for you. It is wonderful, Tom Virtue making the offer; and I take it as a great personal compliment, for he certainly is not what is generally called a lady's man. It is very nice, too, of him to think of my having another lady on board. Whom shall we ask? Oh, I know," she said suddenly; "that will be the thing of all others. We will ask my cousin Minnie; she is full of fun and life, and will make a charming wife for Tom!"

James Grantham laughed.

"What schemers you all are, Fanny! Now I should call it downright treachery to take anyone on board the Seabird with the idea of capturing its master."

"Nonsense, treachery!" Mrs. Grantham said indignantly; "Minnie is the nicest girl I know, and it would do Tom a world of good to have a wife to look after him. Why, he is thirty now, and will be settling down into a confirmed old bachelor before long. It's the greatest kindness we could do him, to take Minnie on board; and I am sure he is the sort of man any girl might fall in love with when she gets to know him. The fact is, he's shy! He never had any sisters, and spends all his time in winter at that horrid club; so that really he has never had any women's society, and even with us he will never come unless he knows we are alone. I call it a great pity, for I don't know a pleasanter fellow than he is. I think it will be doing him a real service in asking Minnie; so that's settled. I will sit down and write him a note."

"In for a penny, in for a pound, I suppose," was Tom Virtue's comment when he received Mrs. Grantham's letter, thanking him warmly for the invitation, and saying that she would bring her cousin, Miss Graham, with her, if that young lady was disengaged.

As a matter of self defense he at once invited Jack Harvey, who was a mutual friend of himself and Grantham, to be of the party.

"Jack can help Grantham to amuse the women," he said to himself; "that will be more in his line than mine. I will run down to Cowes tomorrow and have a chat with Johnson; we shall want a different sort of stores altogether from those we generally carry, and I suppose we must do her up a bit below."

Having made up his mind to the infliction of female passengers, Tom Virtue did it handsomely, and when the party came on board at Ryde they were delighted with the aspect of the yacht below. She had been repainted, the saloon and ladies' cabin were decorated in delicate shades of gray, picked out with gold; and the upholsterer, into whose hands the owner of the Seabird had placed her, had done his work with taste and judgment, and the ladies' cabin resembled a little boudoir.

"Why, Tom, I should have hardly known her!" Grantham, who had often spent a day on board the Seabird, said.

"I hardly know her myself," Tom said, rather ruefully; "but I hope she's all right, Mrs. Grantham, and that you and Miss Graham will find everything you want."

"It is charming!" Mrs. Grantham said enthusiastically. "It's awfully good of you, Tom, and we appreciate it; don't we, Minnie? It is such a surprise, too; for James said that while I should find everything very comfortable, I must not expect that a small yacht would be got up like a palace."

So a fortnight had passed; they had cruised along the coast as far as Plymouth, anchoring at night at the various ports on the way. Then they had returned to Southampton, and it had been settled that as none of the party, with the exception of Virtue himself, had been to the Channel Islands, the last fortnight of the trip should be spent there. The weather had been delightful, save that there had been some deficiency in wind, and throughout the cruise the Seabird had been under all the sail she could spread. But when the gentlemen came on deck early in the morning a considerable change had taken place; the sky was gray and the clouds flying fast overhead.

"We are going to have dirty weather," Tom Virtue said at once. "I don't think it's going to be a gale, but there will be more sea on than will be pleasant for ladies. I tell you what, Grantham; the best thing will be for you to go on shore with the two ladies, and cross by the boat tonight. If you don't mind going directly after breakfast I will start at once, and shall be at St. Helier's as soon as you are."

And so it had been agreed, but not, as has been seen, without opposition and protest on the part of the ladies.

Mrs. Grantham's chief reason for objecting had not been given. The little scheme on which she had set her mind seemed to be working satisfactorily. From the first day Tom Virtue had exerted himself to play the part of host satisfactorily, and had ere long shaken off any shyness he may have felt towards the one stranger of the party, and he and Miss Graham had speedily got on friendly terms. So things were going on as well as Mrs. Grantham could have expected.

No sooner had his guests left the side of the yacht than her owner began to make his preparations for a start.

"What do you think of the weather, Watkins?" he asked his skipper.

"It's going to blow hard, sir; that's my view of it, and if I was you I shouldn't up anchor today. Still, it's just as you likes; the Seabird won't mind it if we don't. She has had a rough time of it before now; still, it will be a case of wet jackets, and no mistake."

"Yes, I expect we shall have a rough time of it, Watkins, but I want to get across. We don't often let ourselves be weather bound, and I am not going to begin it today. We had better house the topmast at once, and get two reefs in the mainsail. We can get the other down when we get clear of the island. Get number three jib up, and the leg of mutton mizzen; put two reefs in the foresail."

Tom and his friend Harvey, who was a good sailor, assisted the crew in reefing down the sails, and a few minutes after the gig had returned and been hoisted in, the yawl was running rapidly down Southampton waters.

"We need hardly have reefed quite so closely," Jack Harvey said, as he puffed away at his pipe.

"Not yet, Jack; but you will see she has as much as she can carry before long. It's all the better to make all snug before starting; it saves a lot of trouble afterwards, and the extra canvas would not have made ten minutes' difference to us at the outside. We shall have pretty nearly a dead beat down the Solent. Fortunately the tide will be running strong with us, but there will be a nasty kick up there. You will see we shall feel the short choppy seas there more than we shall when we get outside. She is a grand boat in a really heavy sea, but in short waves she puts her nose into it with a will. Now, if you will take my advice, you will do as I am going to do; put on a pair of fisherman's boots and oilskin and sou'wester. There are several sets for you to choose from below."

As her owner had predicted, the Seabird put her bowsprit under pretty frequently in the Solent; the wind was blowing half a gale, and as it met the tide it knocked up a short, angry sea, crested with white heads, and Jack Harvey agreed that she had quite as much sail on her as she wanted. The cabin doors were bolted, and all made snug to prevent the water getting below before they got to the race off Hurst Castle; and it was well that they did so, for she was as much under water as she was above.

"I think if I had given way to the ladies and brought them with us they would have changed their minds by this time, Jack," Tom Virtue said, with a laugh.

"I should think so," his friend agreed; "this is not a day for a fair weather sailor. Look what a sea is breaking on the shingles!"

"Yes, five minutes there would knock her into matchwood. Another ten minutes and we shall be fairly out; and I shan't be sorry; one feels as if one was playing football, only just at present the Seabird is the ball and the waves the kickers."

Another quarter of an hour and they had passed the Needles.

"That is more pleasant, Jack," as the short, chopping motion was exchanged for a regular rise and fall; "this is what I enjoy—a steady wind and a regular sea. The Seabird goes over it like one of her namesakes; she is not taking a teacupful now over her bows.

"Watkins, you may as well take the helm for a spell, while we go down to lunch. I am not sorry to give it up for a bit, for it has been jerking like the kick of a horse.

"That's right, Jack, hang up your oilskin there. Johnson, give us a couple of towels; we have been pretty well smothered up there on deck. Now what have you got for us?"

"There is some soup ready, sir, and that cold pie you had for dinner yesterday."

"That will do; open a couple of bottles of stout."

Lunch over, they went on deck again.

"She likes a good blow as well as we do," Virtue said enthusiastically, as the yawl rose lightly over each wave. "What do you think of it, Watkins? Is the wind going to lull a bit as the sun goes down?"

"I think not, sir. It seems to me it's blowing harder than it was."

"Then we will prepare for the worst, Watkins; get the trysail up on deck. When you are ready we will bring her up into the wind and set it. That's the comfort of a yawl, Jack; one can always lie to without any bother, and one hasn't got such a tremendous boom to handle."

The trysail was soon on deck, and then the Seabird was brought up into the wind, the weather foresheet hauled aft, the mizzen sheeted almost fore and aft, and the Seabird lay, head to wind, rising and falling with a gentle motion, in strong contrast to her impetuous rushes when under sail.

"She would ride out anything like that," her owner said. "Last time we came through the Bay on our way from Gib. we were caught in a gale strong enough to blow the hair off one's head, and we lay to for nearly three days, and didn't ship a bucket of water all the time. Now let us lend a hand to get the mainsail stowed."

Ten minutes' work and it was securely fastened and its cover on; two reefs were put in the trysail. Two hands went to each of the halliards, while, as the sail rose, Tom Virtue fastened the toggles round the mast.

"All ready, Watkins?"

"All ready, sir."

"Slack off the weather foresheet, then, and haul aft the leeward. Slack out the mizzen sheet a little, Jack. That's it; now she's off again, like a duck."

The Seabird felt the relief from the pressure of the heavy boom to leeward and rose easily and lightly over the waves.

"She certainly is a splendid seaboat, Tom; I don't wonder you are ready to go anywhere in her. I thought we were rather fools for starting this morning, although I enjoy a good blow; but now I don't care how hard it comes on."

By night it was blowing a downright gale.

"We will lie to till morning, Watkins. So that we get in by daylight tomorrow evening, that is all we want. See our side lights are burning well, and you had better get up a couple of blue lights, in case anything comes running up Channel and don't see our lights. We had better divide into two watches; I will keep one with Matthews and Dawson, Mr. Harvey will go in your watch with Nicholls. We had better get the trysail down altogether, and lie to under the foresail and mizzen, but don't put many lashings on the trysail, one will be enough, and have it ready to cast off in a moment, in case we want to hoist the sail in a hurry. I will go down and have a glass of hot grog first, and then I will take my watch to begin with. Let the two hands with me go down; the steward will serve them out a tot each. Jack, you had better turn in at once."

Virtue was soon on deck again, muffled up in his oilskins.

"Now, Watkins, you can go below and turn in."

"I shan't go below tonight, sir—not to lie down. There's nothing much to do here, but I couldn't sleep, if I did lie down."

"Very well; you had better go below and get a glass of grog; tell the steward to give you a big pipe with a cover like this, out of the locker; and there's plenty of chewing tobacco, if the men are short."

"I will take that instead of a pipe," Watkins said; "there's nothing like a quid in weather like this, it aint never in your way, and it lasts. Even with a cover a pipe would soon be out."

"Please yourself, Watkins; tell the two hands forward to keep a bright lookout for lights."

The night passed slowly. Occasionally a sea heavier than usual came on board, curling over the bow and falling with a heavy thud on the deck, but for the most part the Seabird breasted the waves easily; the bowsprit had been reefed in to its fullest, thereby adding to the lightness and buoyancy of the boat. Tom Virtue did not go below when his friend came up to relieve him at the change of watch, but sat smoking and doing much talking in the short intervals between the gusts.

The morning broke gray and misty, driving sleet came along on the wind, and the horizon was closed in as by a dull curtain.

"How far can we see, do you think, Watkins?"

"Perhaps a couple of miles, sir."

"That will be enough. I think we both know the position of every reef to within a hundred yards, so we will shape our course for Guernsey. If we happen to hit it off, we can hold on to St. Helier, but if when we think we ought to be within sight of Guernsey we see nothing of it, we must lie to again, till the storm has blown itself out or the clouds lift. It would never do to go groping our way along with such currents as run among the islands. Put the last reef in the trysail before you hoist it. I think you had better get the foresail down altogether, and run up the spitfire jib."

The Seabird was soon under way again.

"Now, Watkins, you take the helm; we will go down and have a cup of hot coffee, and I will see that the steward has a good supply for you and the hands; but first, do you take the helm, Jack, whilst Watkins and I have a look at the chart, and try and work out where we are, and the course we had better lie for Guernsey."

Five minutes were spent over the chart, then Watkins went above and Jack Harvey came below.

"You have got the coffee ready, I hope, Johnson?"

"Yes, sir, coffee and chocolate. I didn't know which you would like."

"Chocolate, by all means. Jack, I recommend the chocolate. Bring two full sized bowls, Johnson, and put that cold pie on the table, and a couple of knives and forks; never mind about a cloth; but first of all bring a couple of basins of hot water, we shall enjoy our food more after a wash."

The early breakfast was eaten, dry coats and mufflers put on, pipes lighted, and they then went up upon deck. Tom took the helm.

"What time do you calculate we ought to make Guernsey, Tom?"

"About twelve. The wind is freer than it was, and we are walking along at a good pace. Matthews, cast the log, and let's see what we are doing. About seven knots, I should say."

"Seven and a quarter, sir," the man said, when he checked the line.

"Not a bad guess, Tom; it's always difficult to judge pace in a heavy sea."

At eleven o'clock the mist ceased.

"That's fortunate," Tom Virtue said; "I shouldn't be surprised if we get a glimpse of the sun between the clouds presently. Will you get my sextant and the chronometer up, Jack, and put them handy?"

Jack Harvey did as he was asked, but there was no occasion to use the instruments, for ten minutes later, Watkins, who was standing near the bow gazing fixedly ahead, shouted:

"There's Guernsey, sir, on her lee bow, about six miles away, I should say."

"That's it, sure enough," Tom agreed, as he gazed in the direction in which Watkins was pointing. "There's a gleam of sunshine on it, or we shouldn't have seen it yet. Yes, I think you are about right as to the distance. Now let us take its bearings, we may lose it again directly."

Having taken the bearings of the island they went below, and marked off their position on the chart, and they shaped their course for Cape Grosnez, the northwestern point of Jersey. The gleam of sunshine was transient—the clouds closed in again overhead, darker and grayer than before. Soon the drops of rain came flying before the wind, the horizon closed in, and they could not see half a mile away, but, though the sea was heavy, the Seabird was making capital weather of it, and the two friends agreed that, after all, the excitement of a sail like this was worth a month of pottering about in calms.

"We must keep a bright lookout presently," the skipper said; "there are some nasty rocks off the coast of Jersey. We must give them a wide berth. We had best make round to the south of the island, and lay to there till we can pick up a pilot to take us into St. Helier. I don't think it will be worth while trying to get into St. Aubyn's Bay by ourselves."

"I think so, too, Watkins, but we will see what it is like before it gets dark; if we can pick up a pilot all the better; if not, we will lie to till morning, if the weather keeps thick; but if it clears so that we can make out all the lights we ought to be able to get into the bay anyhow."

An hour later the rain ceased and the sky appeared somewhat clearer. Suddenly Watkins exclaimed, "There is a wreck, sir! There, three miles away to leeward. She is on the Paternosters."

"Good Heavens! she is a steamer," Tom exclaimed, as he caught sight of her the next time the Seabird lifted on a wave. "Can she be the Southampton boat, do you think?"

"Like enough, sir, she may have had it thicker than we had, and may not have calculated enough for the current."

"Up helm, Jack, and bear away towards her. Shall we shake out a reef, Watkins?"

"I wouldn't, sir; she has got as much as she can carry on her now. We must mind what we are doing, sir; the currents run like a millstream, and if we get that reef under our lee, and the wind and current both setting us on to it, it will be all up with us in no time."

"Yes, I know that, Watkins. Jack, take the helm a minute while we run down and look at the chart.

"Our only chance, Watkins, is to work up behind the reef, and try and get so that they can either fasten a line to a buoy and let it float down to us, or get into a boat, if they have one left, and drift to us."

"They are an awful group of rocks," Watkins said, as they examined the chart; "you see some of them show merely at high tide, and a lot of them are above at low water. It will be an awful business to get among them rocks, sir, just about as near certain death as a thing can be."

"Well, it's got to be done, Watkins," Tom said firmly. "I see the danger as well as you do, but whatever the risk it must be tried. Mr. Grantham and the two ladies went on board by my persuasion, and I should never forgive myself if anything happened to them. But I will speak to the men."

He went on deck again and called the men to him. "Look here, lads; you see that steamer ashore on the Paternosters. In such a sea as this she may go to pieces in half an hour. I am determined to make an effort to save the lives of those on board. As you can see for yourselves there is no lying to weather of her, with the current and wind driving us on to the reef; we must beat up from behind. Now, lads, the sea there is full of rocks, and the chances are ten to one we strike on to them and go to pieces; but, anyhow, I am going to try; but I won't take you unless you are willing. The boat is a good one, and the zinc chambers will keep her afloat if she fills; well managed, you ought to be able to make the coast of Jersey in her. Mr. Harvey, Watkins, and I can handle the yacht, so you can take the boat if you like."

The men replied that they would stick to the yacht wherever Mr. Virtue chose to take her, and muttered something about the ladies, for the pleasant faces of Mrs. Grantham and Miss Graham had, during the fortnight they had been on board, won the men's hearts.

"Very well, lads, I am glad to find you will stick by me; if we pull safely through it I will give each of you three months' wages. Now set to work with a will and get the gig out. We will tow her after us, and take to her if we make a smash of it."

They were now near enough to see the white breakers, in the middle of which the ship was lying. She was fast breaking up. The jagged outline showed that the stern had been beaten in. The masts and funnel were gone, and the waves seemed to make a clean breach over her, almost hiding her from sight in a white cloud of spray.

"Wood and iron can't stand that much longer," Jack Harvey said; "another hour and I should say there won't be two planks left together."

"It is awful, Jack; I would give all I have in the world if I had not persuaded them to go on board. Keep her off a little more, Watkins."

The Seabird passed within a cable's length of the breakers at the northern end of the reef.

"Now, lads, take your places at the sheets, ready to haul or let go as I give the word." So saying, Tom Virtue took his place in the bow, holding on by the forestay.

Among Malay Pirates

The wind was full on the Seabird's beam as she entered the broken water. Here and there the dark heads of the rocks showed above the water. These were easy enough to avoid, the danger lay in those hidden beneath its surface, and whose position was indicated only by the occasional break of a sea as it passed over them. Every time the Seabird sank on a wave those on board involuntarily held their breath, but the water here was comparatively smooth, the sea having spent its first force upon the outer reef. With a wave of his hand Tom directed the helmsman as to his course, and the little yacht was admirably handled through the dangers.

"I begin to think we shall do it," Tom said to Jack Harvey, who was standing close to him. "Another five minutes and we shall be within reach of her."

It could be seen now that there was a group of people clustered in the bow of the wreck. Two or three light lines were coiled in readiness for throwing.

"Now, Watkins," Tom said, going aft, "make straight for the wreck. I see no broken water between us and them, and possibly there may be deep water under their bow."

It was an anxious moment, as, with the sails flattened in, the yawl forged up nearly in the eye of the wind towards the wreck. Her progress was slow, for she was now stemming the current.

Tom stood with a coil of line in his hand in the bow.

"You get ready to throw, Jack, if I miss."

Nearer and nearer the yacht approached the wreck, until the bowsprit of the latter seemed to stand almost over her. Then Tom threw the line. It fell over the bowsprit, and a cheer broke from those on board the wreck and from the sailors of the Seabird. A stronger line was at once fastened to that thrown, and to this a strong hawser was attached.

"Down with the helm, Watkins. Now, lads, lower away the trysail as fast as you can. Now, one of you, clear that hawser as they haul on it. Now out with the anchors."

These had been got into readiness; it was not thought that they would get any hold on the rocky bottom, still they might catch on a projecting ledge, and at any rate their weight and that of the chain cable would relieve the strain upon the hawser.

Two sailors had run out on the bowsprit of the wreck as soon as the line was thrown, and the end of the hawser was now on board the steamer.

"Thank God, there's Grantham!" Jack Harvey exclaimed; "do you see him waving his hand?"

"I see him," Tom said, "but I don't see the ladies."

"They are there, no doubt," Jack said confidently; "crouching down, I expect. He would not be there if they weren't, you may be sure. Yes, there they are; those two muffled up figures. There, one of them has thrown back her cloak and is waving her arm."

The two young men waved their caps.

"Are the anchors holding, Watkins? There's a tremendous strain on that hawser."

"I think so, sir; they are both tight."

"Put them round the windlass, and give a turn or two, we must relieve the strain on that hawser."

Since they had first seen the wreck the waves had made great progress in the work of destruction, and the steamer had broken in two just aft of the engines.

"Get over the spare spars, Watkins, and fasten them to float in front of her bows like a triangle. Matthews, catch hold of that boat hook and try to fend off any piece of timber that comes along. You get hold of the sweeps, lads, and do the same. They would stave her in like a nutshell if they struck her."

"Thank God, here comes the first of them!"

Those on board the steamer had not been idle. As soon as the yawl was seen approaching slings were prepared, and no sooner was the hawser securely fixed, than the slings were attached to it and a woman placed in them. The hawser was tight and the descent sharp, and without a check the figure ran down to the deck of the Seabird. She was lifted out of the slings by Tom and Jack Harvey, who found she was an old woman and had entirely lost consciousness.

"Two of you carry her down below; tell Johnson to pour a little brandy down her throat. Give her some hot soup as soon as she comes to."

Another woman was lowered and helped below. The next to descend was Mrs. Grantham.

"Thank God, you are rescued!" Tom said, as he helped her out of the sling.

"Thank God, indeed," Mrs. Grantham said, "and thank you all! Oh, Tom, we have had a terrible time of it, and had lost all hope till we saw your sail, and even then the captain said that he was afraid nothing could be done. Minnie was the first to make out it was you, and then we began to hope. She has been so brave, dear girl. Ah! here she comes."

But Minnie's firmness came to an end now that she felt the need for it was over. She was unable to stand when she was lifted from the slings, and Tom carried her below.

"Are there any more women, Mrs. Grantham?"

"No; there was only one other lady passenger and the stewardess."

"Then you had better take possession of your own cabin. I ordered Johnson to spread a couple more mattresses and some bedding on the floor, so you will all four be able to turn in. There's plenty of hot coffee and soup. I should advise soup with two or three spoonfuls of brandy in it. Now, excuse me; I must go upon deck."

Twelve men descended by the hawser, one of them with both legs broken by the fall of the mizzen. The last to come was the captain.

"Is that all?" Tom asked.

"That is all," the captain said. "Six men were swept overboard when she first struck, and two were killed by the fall of the funnel. Fortunately we had only three gentlemen passengers and three ladies on board. The weather looked so wild when we started that no one else cared about making the passage. God bless you, sir, for what you have done! Another half hour and it would have been all over with us. But it seems like a miracle your getting safe through the rocks to us."

Among Malay Pirates

"It was fortunate indeed that we came along," Tom said; "three of the passengers are dear friends of mine; and as it was by my persuasion that they came across in the steamer instead of in the yacht, I should never have forgiven myself if they had been lost. Take all your men below, captain; you will find plenty of hot soup there. Now, Watkins, let us be off; that steamer won't hold together many minutes longer, so there's no time to lose. We will go back as we came. Give me a hatchet. Now, lads, two of you stand at the chain cables; knock out the shackles the moment I cut the hawser. Watkins, you take the helm and let her head pay off till the jib fills. Jack, you lend a hand to the other two, and get up the trysail again as soon as we are free."

In a moment all were at their stations. The helm was put on the yacht, and she payed off on the opposite tack to that on which she had before been sailing. As soon as the jib filled, Tom gave two vigorous blows with his hatchet on the hawser, and, as he lifted his hand for a third, it parted. Then came the sharp rattle of the chains as they ran round the hawser holes. The trysail was hoisted and sheeted home, and the Seabird was under way again. Tom, as before, conned the ship from the bow. Several times she was in close proximity to the rocks, but each time she avoided them. A shout of gladness rose from all on deck as she passed the last patch of white water. Then she tacked and bore away for Jersey.

Tom had now time to go down below and look after his passengers. They consisted of the captain and two sailors—the sole survivors of those who had been on deck when the vessel struck—three male passengers, and six engineers and stokers.

"I have not had time to shake you by the hand before, Tom," Grantham said, as Tom Virtue entered; "and I thought you would not want me on deck at present. God bless you, old fellow! We all owe you our lives."

"How did it happen, captain?" Tom asked, as the captain also came up to him.

"It was the currents, I suppose," the captain said; "it was so thick we could not see a quarter of a mile any way. The weather was so wild I would not put into Guernsey, and passed the island without seeing it. I steered my usual course, but the gale must have altered the currents, for I thought I was three miles away from the reef, when we saw it on our beam, not a hundred yards away. It was too late to avoid it then, and in another minute we ran upon it, and the waves were sweeping over us. Everyone behaved well. I got all, except those who had been swept overboard or crushed by the funnel, up into the bow of the ship, and there we waited. There was nothing to be done. No boat would live for a moment in the sea on that reef, and all I could advise was that when she went to pieces everyone should try to get hold of a floating fragment; but I doubt whether a man would have been alive a quarter of an hour after she went to pieces."

"Perhaps, captain, you will come on deck with me and give me the benefit of your advice. My skipper and I know the islands pretty well, but no doubt you know them a good deal better, and I don't want another mishap."

But the Seabird avoided all further dangers, and as it became dark the lights of St. Helier's were in sight, and an hour later the yacht brought up in the port and landed her involuntary passengers.

A fortnight afterwards the Seabird returned to England, and two months later Mrs. Grantham had the satisfaction of being present at the ceremony which was the successful consummation of her little scheme in inviting Minnie Graham to be her companion on board the Seabird.

"Well, my dear," her husband said, when she indulged in a little natural triumph, "I do not say that it has not turned out well, and I am heartily glad for both Tom and Minnie's sake it has so; but you must allow that it very nearly had a disastrous ending, and I think if I were you I should leave matters to take their natural course in future. I have accepted Tom's invitation for the same party to take a cruise in the Seabird next summer, but I have bargained that next time a storm is brewing up we shall stop quietly in port."

"That's all very well, James," Mrs. Grantham said saucily; "but you must remember that Tom Virtue will only be first mate of the Seabird in future."

"That I shall be able to tell you better, my dear, after our next cruise. All husbands are not as docile and easily led as I am."

A Pipe Of Mystery

A jovial party were gathered round a blazing fire in an old grange near Warwick. The hour was getting late; the very little ones had, after dancing round the Christmas tree, enjoying the snapdragon, and playing a variety of games, gone off to bed; and the elder boys and girls now gathered round their uncle, Colonel Harley, and asked him for a story—above all, a ghost story.

"But I have never seen any ghosts," the colonel said, laughing; "and, moreover, I don't believe in them one bit. I have traveled pretty well all over the world, I have slept in houses said to be haunted, but nothing have I seen—no noises that could not be accounted for by rats or the wind have I ever heard. I have never "—and here he paused—"never but once met with any circumstances or occurrence that could not be accounted for by the light of reason, and I know you prefer hearing stories of my own adventures to mere invention."

"Yes, uncle. But what was the 'once' when circumstances happened that you could not explain?"

"It's rather a long story," the colonel said, "and it's getting late."

"Oh! no, no, uncle; it does not matter a bit how late we sit up on Christmas Eve, and the longer the story is, the better; and if you don't believe in ghosts how can it be a story of something you could not account for by the light of nature?"

"You will see when I have done," the colonel said. "It is rather a story of what the Scotch call second sight, than one of ghosts. As to accounting for it, you shall form your own opinion when you have heard me to the end.

"I landed in India in '50, and after going through the regular drill work marched with a detachment up country to join my regiment, which was stationed at Jubbalpore, in the very heart of India. It has become an important place since; the railroad across India passes through it and no end of changes have taken place; but at that time it was one of the most out of the way stations in India, and, I may say, one of the most pleasant. It lay high, there was capital boating on the Nerbudda, and, above all, it was a grand place for sport, for it lay at the foot of the hill country, an immense district, then but little known, covered with forests and jungle, and abounding with big game of all kinds.

"My great friend there was a man named Simmonds. He was just of my own standing; we had come out in the same ship, had marched up the country together, and were almost like brothers. He was an old Etonian, I an old Westminster, and we were both fond of boating, and, indeed, of sport of all kinds. But I am not going to tell you of that now. The people in these hills are called Gonds, a true hill tribe—that is to say, aborigines, somewhat of the negro type. The chiefs are of mixed blood, but the people are almost black. They are supposed to accept the religion of the Hindus, but are in reality deplorably ignorant and superstitious. Their priests are a sort of compound of a Brahmin priest and a negro fetish man, and among their principal duties is that of charming away tigers from the villages by means of incantations. There, as in other parts of India, were a few wandering fakirs, who enjoyed an immense reputation for holiness and wisdom. The people would go to them from great distances for charms or predictions, and believed in their power with implicit faith.

"At the time when we were at Jubbalpore there was one of these fellows whose reputation altogether eclipsed that of his rivals, and nothing could be done until his permission had been asked and his blessing obtained. All sorts of marvelous stories were constantly coming to our ears of the unerring foresight with which he predicted the termination of diseases, both in men and animals; and so generally was he believed in that the colonel ordered that no one connected with the regiment should consult him, for these predictions very frequently brought about their own fulfillment; for those who were told that an illness would terminate fatally, lost all hope, and literally lay down to die.

"However, many of the stories that we heard could not be explained on these grounds, and the fakir and his doings were often talked over at mess, some of the officers scoffing at the whole business, others maintaining that some of these fakirs had, in some way or another, the power of foretelling the future, citing many well authenticated anecdotes upon the subject.

"The older officers were the believers, we young fellows were the scoffers. But for the well known fact that it is very seldom indeed that these fakirs will utter any of their predictions to Europeans, some of us would have gone to him to test his powers. As it was, none of us had ever seen him.

"He lived in an old ruined temple, in the middle of a large patch of jungle at the foot of the hills, some ten or twelve miles away.

"I had been at Jubbalpore about a year, when I was woke up one night by a native, who came in to say that at about eight o'clock a tiger had killed a man in his village, and had dragged off the body.

"Simmonds and I were constantly out after tigers, and the people in all the villages within twenty miles knew that we were always ready to pay for early information. This tiger had been doing great damage, and had carried off about thirty men, women, and children. So great was the fear of him, indeed, that the people in the neighborhood he frequented scarcely dared stir out of doors, except in parties of five or six. We had had several hunts after him, but, like all man eaters, he was old and awfully crafty; and although we got several snap shots at him, he had always managed to save his skin.

"In a quarter of an hour after the receipt of the message Charley Simmonds and I were on the back of an elephant which was our joint property; our shikaree, a capital fellow, was on foot beside us, and with the native trotting on ahead as guide we went off at the best pace of old Begaum, for that was the elephant's name. The village was fifteen miles away, but we got there soon after daybreak, and were received with delight by the population. In half an hour the hunt was organized; all the male population turned out as beaters, with sticks, guns, tom-toms, and other instruments for making a noise.

"The trail was not difficult to find. A broad path, with occasional smears of blood, showed where he had dragged his victim through the long grass to a cluster of trees a couple of hundred yards from the village.

"We scarcely expected to find him there, but the villagers held back, while we went forward with cocked rifles. We found, however, nothing but a few bones and a quantity of blood. The tiger had made off at the approach of daylight into the jungle, which was about two miles distant. We traced him easily enough, and found that he had entered a large ravine, from which several smaller ones branched off.

"It was an awkward place, as it was next to impossible to surround it with the number of people at our command. We posted them at last all along the upper ground, and told them to make up in noise what they wanted in numbers. At last all was ready, and we gave the signal. However, I am not telling you a hunting story, and need only say that we could neither find nor disturb him. In vain we pushed Begaum through the thickest of the jungle which clothed the sides and bottom of the ravine, while the men shouted, beat their tom-toms, and showered imprecations against the tiger himself and his ancestors up to the remotest generations.

"The day was tremendously hot, and, after three hours' march, we gave it up for a time, and lay down in the shade, while the shikarees made a long examination of the ground all round the hillside, to be sure that he had not left the ravine. They came back with the news that no traces could be discovered, and that, beyond a doubt, he was still there. A tiger will crouch up in an exceedingly small clump of grass or bush, and will sometimes almost allow himself to be trodden on before moving. However, we determined to have one more search, and if that should prove unsuccessful, to send off to Jubbalpore for some more of the men to come out with elephants, while we kept up a circle of fires, and of noises of all descriptions, so as to keep him a prisoner until the arrival of the reinforcements. Our next search was no more successful than our first had been; and having, as we imagined, examined every clump and crevice in which he could have been concealed, we had just reached the upper end of the ravine, when we heard a tremendous roar, followed by a perfect babel of yells and screams from the natives.

"The outburst came from the mouth of the ravine, and we felt at once that he had escaped. We hurried back to find, as we had expected, that the tiger was gone. He had burst out suddenly from his hiding place, had seized a native, torn him horribly, and had made across the open plain.

"This was terribly provoking, but we had nothing to do but follow him. This was easy enough, and we traced him to a detached patch of wood and jungle, two miles distant. This wood was four or five hundred yards across, and the exclamations of the people at once told us that it was the one in which stood the ruined temple of the fakir of whom I have been telling you. I forgot to say that as the tiger broke out one of the village shikarees had fired at and, he declared, wounded him.

"It was already getting late in the afternoon, and it was hopeless to attempt to beat the jungle that night. We therefore sent off a runner with a note to the colonel, asking him to send the work elephants, and to allow a party of volunteers to march over at night, to help surround the jungle when we commenced beating it in the morning.

"We based our request upon the fact that the tiger was a notorious man eater, and had been doing immense damage. We then had a talk with our shikaree, sent a man off to bring provisions for the people out with us, and then set them to work cutting dry sticks and grass to make a circle of fires.

"We both felt much uneasiness respecting the fakir, who might be seized at any moment by the enraged tiger. The natives would not allow that there was any cause for fear, as the tiger would not dare to touch so holy a man. Our belief in the respect of the tiger for sanctity was by no means strong, and we determined to go in and warn him of the presence of the brute in the wood. It was a mission which we could not intrust to anyone else, for no native would have entered the jungle for untold gold; so we mounted the Begaum again, and started. The path leading towards the temple was pretty wide, and as we went along almost noiselessly, for the elephant was too well trained to tread upon fallen sticks, it was just possible we might come upon the tiger suddenly, so we kept our rifles in readiness in our hands.

"Presently we came in sight of the ruins. No one was at first visible; but at that very moment the fakir came out from the temple. He could not see or hear us, for we were rather behind him and still among the trees, but at once proceeded in a high voice to break into a singsong prayer. He had not said two words before his voice was drowned in a terrific roar, and in an instant the tiger had sprung upon him, struck him to the ground, seized him as a cat would a mouse, and started off with him at a trot. The brute evidently had not detected our presence, for he came right towards us. We halted the Begaum, and, with our fingers on the triggers, awaited the favorable moment. He was a hundred yards from us when he struck down his victim; he was not more than fifty when he caught sight of us. He stopped for an instant in surprise. Charley muttered, 'Both barrels, Harley,' and as the beast turned to plunge into the jungle, and so showed us his side, we sent four bullets crashing into him, and he rolled over lifeless.

"We went up to the spot, made the Begaum give him a kick, to be sure that he was dead, and then got down to examine the unfortunate fakir. The tiger had seized him by the shoulder, which was terribly torn, and the bone broken. He was still perfectly conscious.

"We at once fired three shots, our usual signal that the tiger was dead, and in a few minutes were surrounded by the villagers, who hardly knew whether to be delighted at the death of their enemy, or to grieve over the injury to the fakir. We proposed taking the latter to our hospital at Jubbalpore, but this he positively refused to listen to. However, we finally persuaded him to allow his arm to be set and the wounds dressed in the first place by our regimental surgeon, after which he could go to one of the native villages and have his arm dressed in accordance with his own notions. A litter was soon improvised, and away we went to Jubbalpore, which we reached about eight in the evening.

"The fakir refused to enter the hospital, so we brought out a couple of trestles, laid the litter upon them, and the surgeon set his arm and dressed his wounds by torchlight, when he was lifted into a dhoolie, and his bearers again prepared to start for the village.

"Hitherto he had only spoken a few words; but he now briefly expressed his deep gratitude to Simmonds and myself. We told him that we would ride over to see him shortly, and hoped to find him getting on rapidly. Another minute and he was gone.

"It happened that we had three or four fellows away on leave or on staff duty, and several others laid up with fever just about this time, so that the duty fell very heavily upon the rest of us, and it was over a month before we had time to ride over to see the fakir.

"We had heard he was going on well; but we were surprised, on reaching the village, to find that he had already returned to his old abode in the jungle. However, we had made up our minds to see him, especially as we had agreed that we would endeavor to persuade him to do a prediction for us; so we turned our horses' heads towards the jungle. We found the fakir sitting on a rock in front of the temple, just where he had been seized by the tiger. He rose as we rode up.

"'I knew that you would come today, sahibs, and was joyful in the thought of seeing those who have preserved my life.'

"'We are glad to see you looking pretty strong again, though your arm is still in a sling,' I said, for Simmonds was not strong in Hindustani.

"'How did you know that we were coming?' I asked, when we had tied up our horses.

"'Siva has given to his servant to know many things,' he said quietly.

"'Did you know beforehand that the tiger was going to seize you?' I asked.

"'I knew that a great danger threatened, and that Siva would not let me die before my time had come.'

"'Could you see into our future?' I asked.

"The fakir hesitated, looked at me for a moment earnestly to see if I was speaking in mockery, and then said:

"'The sahibs do not believe in the power of Siva or of his servants.. They call his messengers imposters, and scoff at them when they speak of the events of the future.'

"'No indeed,' I said. 'My friend and I have no idea of scoffing. We have heard of so many of your predictions coming true, that we are really anxious that you should tell us something of the future.'

"The fakir nodded his head, went into the temple, and returned in a minute or two with two small pipes used by the natives for opium smoking, and a brazier of burning charcoal. The pipes were already charged. He made signs to us to sit down, and took his place in front of us. Then he began singing in a low voice, rocking himself to and fro, and waving a staff which he held in his hand. Gradually his voice rose, and his gesticulations and actions became more violent. So far as I could make out, it was a prayer to Siva that he would give some glimpse of the future which might benefit the sahibs who had saved the life of his servant. Presently he darted forward, gave us each a pipe, took two pieces of red hot charcoal from the brazier in his fingers, without seeming to know that they were warm, and placed them in the pipes; then he recommenced his singing and gesticulations.

"A glance at Charley, to see if, like myself, he was ready to carry the thing through, and then I put the pipe to my lips. I felt at once that it was opium, of which I had before made experiment, but mixed with some other substance, which was, I imagine, hasheesh, a preparation of hemp. A few puffs, and I felt a drowsiness creeping over me. I saw, as through a mist, the fakir swaying himself backwards and forwards, his arms waving and his face distorted. Another minute, and the pipe slipped from my fingers, and I fell back insensible.

"How long I lay there I do not know. I woke with a strange and not unpleasant sensation, and presently became conscious that the fakir was gently pressing, with a sort of shampooing action, my temples and head. When he saw that I opened my eyes he left me, and performed the same process upon Charley. In a few minutes he rose from his stooping position, waved his hand in token of adieu, and walked slowly back into the temple.

"As he disappeared I sat up; Charley did the same.

"We stared at each other for a minute without speaking, and then Charley said:

"'This is a rum go, and no mistake, old man.'

"'You're right, Charley. My opinion is, we've made fools of ourselves. Let's be off out of this.'

"We staggered to our feet, for we both felt like drunken men, made our way to our horses, poured a mussuk of water over our heads, took a drink of brandy from our flasks, and then, feeling more like ourselves, mounted and rode out of the jungle.

"'Well, Harley, if the glimpse of futurity which I had is true, all I can say is that it was extremely unpleasant.'

"'That was just my case, Charley.'

"'My dream, or whatever you like to call it, was about a mutiny of the men.'

"'You don't say so, Charley; so was mine. This is monstrously strange, to say the least of it. However, you tell your story first, and then I will tell mine.'

"'It was very short,' Charley said. 'We were at mess—not in our present mess room—we were dining with the fellows of some other regiment. Suddenly, without any warning, the windows were filled with a crowd of Sepoys, who opened fire right and left into us. Half the fellows were shot down at once; the rest of us made a rush to our swords just as the niggers came swarming into the room. There was a desperate fight for a moment. I remember that Subadar Piran—one of the best native officers in the regiment, by the way—made a rush at me, and I shot him through the head with a revolver. At the same moment a ball hit me, and down I went. At the moment a Sepoy fell dead across me, hiding me partly from sight. The fight lasted a minute or two longer. I fancy a few fellows escaped, for I heard shots outside. Then the place became quiet. In another minute I heard a crackling, and saw that the devils had set the mess room on fire. One of our men, who was lying close by me, got up and crawled to the window, but he was shot down the moment he showed himself. I was hesitating whether to do the same or to lie still and be smothered, when suddenly I rolled the dead Sepoy off, crawled into the anteroom half suffocated by smoke, raised the lid of a very heavy trapdoor, and stumbled down some steps into a place, half storehouse half cellar, under the mess room. How I knew about it being there I don't know. The trap closed over my head with a bang. That is all I remember.'

"'Well, Charley, curiously enough my dream was also about an extraordinary escape from danger, lasting, like yours, only a minute or two. The first thing I remember—there seems to have been some thing before, but what, I don't know—I was on horseback, holding a very pretty but awfully pale girl in front of me. We were pursued by a whole troop of Sepoy cavalry, who were firing pistol shots at us. We were not more than seventy or eighty yards in front, and they were gaining fast, just as I rode into a large deserted temple. In the center was a huge stone figure. I jumped off my horse with the lady, and as I did so she said, 'blow out my brains, Edward; don't let me fall into their hands.'

"Instead of answering, I hurried her round behind the idol, pushed against one of the leaves of a flower in the carving, and the stone swung back, and showed a hole just large enough to get through, with a stone staircase inside the body of the idol, made, no doubt, for the priest to go up and give responses through the mouth. I hurried the girl through, crept in after her, and closed the stone, just as our pursuers came clattering into the courtyard. That is all I remember.'

"'Well, it is monstrously rum,' Charley said after a pause. 'Did you understand what the old fellow was singing about before he gave us the pipes?'

"'Yes; I caught the general drift. It was an entreaty to Siva to give us some glimpse of futurity which might benefit us.'

"We lit our cheroots and rode for some miles at a brisk canter without remark. When we were within a short distance of home we reined up.

"'I feel ever so much better,' Charley said. 'We have got that opium out of our heads now. How do you account for it all, Harley?'

"'I account for it in this way, Charley. The opium naturally had the effect of making us both dream, and as we took similar doses of the same mixture, under similar circumstances, it is scarcely extraordinary that it should have effected the same portion of the brain, and caused a certain similarity in our dreams. In all nightmares something terrible happens, or is on the point of happening; and so it was here. Not unnaturally in both our cases our thoughts turned to soldiers. If you remember, there was a talk at mess some little time since as to what would happen in the extremely unlikely event of the Sepoys mutinying in a body. I have no doubt that was the foundation of both our dreams. It is all natural enough when we come to think it over calmly. I think, by the way, we had better agree to say nothing at all about it in the regiment.'

"'I should think not,' Charley said. 'We should never hear the end of it; they would chaff us out of our lives.'

"We kept our secret, and came at last to laugh over it heartily when we were together. Then the subject dropped, and by the end of a year had as much escaped our minds as any other dream would have done. Three months after the affair the regiment was ordered down to Allahabad, and the change of place no doubt helped to erase all memory of the dream. Four years after we had left Jubbalpore we went to Beerapore. The time is very marked in my memory, because, the very week we arrived there, your aunt, then Miss Gardiner, came out from England, to her father, our colonel. The instant I saw her I was impressed with the idea that I knew her intimately. I recollected her face, her figure, and the very tone of her voice, but wherever I had met her I could not conceive. Upon the occasion of my first introduction to her I could not help telling her that I was convinced that we had met, and asking her if she did not remember it. No, she did not remember, but very likely she might have done so, and she suggested the names of several people at whose houses we might have met. I did not know any of them. Presently she asked how long I had been out in India?

"'Six years,' I said.

"'And how old, Mr. Harley,' she said, 'do you take me to be?'

"I saw in one instant my stupidity, and was stammering out an apology, when she went on:

"'I am very little over eighteen, Mr. Harley, although I evidently look ever so many years older; but papa can certify to my age; so I was only twelve when you left England.'

"I tried in vain to clear matters up. Your aunt would insist that I took her to be forty, and the fun that my blunder made rather drew us together, and gave me a start over the other fellows at the station, half of whom fell straightway in love with her. Some months went on, and when the mutiny broke out we were engaged to be married. It is a proof of how completely the opium dreams had passed out of the minds of both Simmonds and myself, that even when rumors of general disaffection among the Sepoys began to be current, they never once recurred to us; and even when the news of the actual mutiny reached us we were just as confident as were the others of the fidelity of our own regiment. It was the old story, foolish confidence and black treachery. As at very many other stations, the mutiny broke out when we were at mess. Our regiment was dining with the 34th Bengalees. Suddenly, just as dinner was over, the window was opened, and a tremendous fire poured in. Four or five men fell dead at once, and the poor colonel, who was next to me, was shot right through the head. Everyone rushed to his sword and drew his pistol—for we had been ordered to carry pistols as part of our uniform. I was next to Charley Simmonds as the Sepoys of both regiments, headed by Subadar Piran, poured in at the windows.

"'I have it now,' Charley said; 'it is the scene I dreamed.'

"As he spoke he fired his revolver at the subadar, who fell dead in his tracks.

"A Sepoy close by leveled his musket and fired. Charley fell, and the fellow rushed forward to bayonet him. As he did so I sent a bullet through his head, and he fell across Charley. It was a wild fight for a minute or two, and then a few of us made a sudden rush together, cut our way through the mutineers, and darted through an open window on to the parade. There were shouts, shots, and screams from the officers' bungalows, and in several places flames were already rising. What became of the other men I knew not; I made as hard as I could tear for the colonel's bungalow. Suddenly I came upon a sowar sitting on his horse watching the rising flames. Before he saw me I was on him, and ran him through. I leapt on his horse and galloped down to Gardiner's compound. I saw lots of Sepoys in and around the bungalow, all engaged in looting. I dashed into the compound.

"'May! May!' I shouted. 'Where are you?'

"I had scarcely spoken before a dark figure rushed out of a clump of bushes close by with a scream of delight.

"In an instant she was on the horse before me, and, shooting down a couple of fellows who made a rush at my reins, I dashed out again. Stray shots were fired after us. But fortunately the Sepoys were all busy looting, most of them had laid down their muskets, and no one really took up the pursuit. I turned off from the parade ground, dashed down between the hedges of two compounds, and in another minute we were in the open country.

"Fortunately, the cavalry were all down looting their own lines, or we must have been overtaken at once. May happily had fainted as I lifted her on to my horse—happily, because the fearful screams that we heard from the various bungalows almost drove me mad, and would probably have killed her, for the poor ladies were all her intimate friends.

"I rode on for some hours, till I felt quite safe from any immediate pursuit, and then we halted in the shelter of a clump of trees.

"By this time I had heard May's story. She had felt uneasy at being alone, but had laughed at herself for being so, until upon her speaking to one of the servants he had answered in a tone of gross insolence, which had astonished her. She at once guessed that there was danger, and the moment that she was alone caught up a large, dark carriage rug, wrapped it round her so as to conceal her white dress, and stole out into the veranda. The night was dark, and scarcely had she left the house than she heard a burst of firing across at the mess house. She at once ran in among the bushes and crouched there, as she heard the rush of men into the room she had just left. She heard them searching for her, but they were looking for a white dress, and her dark rug saved her. What she must have suffered in the five minutes between the firing of the first shots and my arrival, she only knows. May had spoken but very little since we started. I believe that she was certain that her father was dead, although I had given an evasive answer when she asked me; and her terrible sense of loss, added to the horror of that time of suspense in the garden, had completely stunned her. We waited in the tope until the afternoon, and then set out again.

"We had gone but a short distance when we saw a body of the rebel cavalry in pursuit. They had no doubt been scouring the country generally, and the discovery was accidental. For a short time we kept away from them, but this could not be for long, as our horse was carrying double. I made for a sort of ruin I saw at the foot of a hill half a mile away. I did so with no idea of the possibility of concealment. My intention was simply to get my back to a rock and to sell my life as dearly as I could, keeping the last two barrels of the revolver for ourselves. Certainly no remembrance of my dream influenced me in any way, and in the wild whirl of excitement I had not given a second thought to Charley Simmonds' exclamation. As we rode up to the ruins only a hundred yards ahead of us, May said:

"'Blow out my brains, Edward; don't let me fall alive into their hands.'

"A shock of remembrance shot across me. The chase, her pale face, the words, the temple—all my dream rushed into my mind.

"'We are saved,' I cried, to her amazement, as we rode into the courtyard, in whose center a great figure was sitting.

"I leapt from the horse, snatched the mussuk of water from the saddle, and then hurried May round the idol, between which and the rock behind there was but just room to get along.

"Not a doubt entered my mind but that I should find the spring as I had dreamed. Sure enough there was the carving, fresh upon my memory as if I had seen it but the day before. I placed my hand on the leaflet without hesitation, a solid stone moved back, I hurried my amazed companion in, and shut to the stone. I found, and shot to a massive bolt, evidently placed to prevent the door being opened by accident or design when anyone was in the idol.

"At first it seemed quite dark, but a faint light streamed in from above; we made our way up the stairs, and found that the light came through a number of small holes pierced in the upper part of the head, and through still smaller holes lower down, not much larger than a good sized knitting needle could pass through. These holes, we afterwards found, were in the ornaments round the idol's neck. The holes enlarged inside, and enabled us to have a view all round.

"The mutineers were furious at our disappearance, and for hours searched about. Then, saying that we must be hidden somewhere, and that they would wait till we came out, they proceeded to bivouac in the courtyard of the temple.

"We passed four terrible days, but on the morning of the fifth a scout came in to tell the rebels that a column of British troops marching on Delhi would pass close by the temple. They therefore hastily mounted and galloped off.

"Three quarters of an hour later we were safe among our own people. A fortnight afterwards your aunt and I were married. It was no time for ceremony then; there were no means of sending her away; no place where she could have waited until the time for her mourning for her father was over. So we were married quietly by one of the chaplains of the troops, and, as your storybooks say, have lived very happily ever after."

"And how about Mr. Simmonds, uncle? Did he get safe off too?"

"Yes, his dream came as vividly to his mind as mine had done. He crawled to the place where he knew the trapdoor would be, and got into the cellar. Fortunately for him there were plenty of eatables there, and he lived there in concealment for a fortnight. After that he crawled out, and found the mutineers had marched for Delhi. He went through a lot, but at last joined us before that city. We often talked over our dreams together, and there was no question that we owed our lives to them. Even then we did not talk much to other people about them, for there would have been a lot of talk, and inquiry, and questions, and you know fellows hate that sort of thing. So we held our tongues. Poor Charley's silence was sealed a year later at Lucknow, for on the advance with Lord Clyde he was killed.

"And now, boys and girls, you must run off to bed. Five minutes more and it will be Christmas Day.

"So you see, Frank, that although I don't believe in ghosts, I have yet met with a circumstance which I cannot account for."

"It is very curious anyhow, uncle, and beats ghost stories into fits."

"I like it better, certainly," one of the girls said, "for we can go to bed without being afraid of dreaming about it."

"Well, you must not talk any more now. Off to bed, off to bed," Colonel Harley said, "or I shall get into terrible disgrace with your fathers and mothers, who have been looking very gravely at me for the last three quarters of an hour."

White Faced Dick: A Story Of Pine Tree Gulch

How Pine Tree Gulch got its name no one knew, for in the early days every ravine and hillside was thickly covered with pines. It may be that a tree of exceptional size caught the eye of the first explorer, that he camped under it, and named the place in its honor; or, maybe, some fallen giant lay in the bottom and hindered the work of the first prospectors. At any rate, Pine Tree Gulch it was, and the name was as good as any other. The pine trees were gone now. Cut up for firing, or for the erection of huts, or the construction of sluices, but the hillside was ragged with their stumps.

The principal camp was at the mouth of the Gulch, where the little stream, which scarce afforded water sufficient for the cradles in the dry season, but which was a rushing torrent in winter, joined the Yuba. The best ground was at the junction of the streams, and lay, indeed, in the Yuba Valley rather than in the Gulch. At first most gold had been found higher up, but there was here comparatively little depth down to the bedrock, and as the ground became exhausted the miners moved down towards the mouth of the Gulch. They were doing well, as a whole, how well no one knew, for miners are chary of giving information as to what they are making; still, it was certain they were doing well, for the bars were doing a roaring trade, and the storekeepers never refused credit—a proof in itself that the prospects were good.

The flat at the mouth of the Gulch was a busy scene, every foot was good paying stuff, for in the eddy, where the torrents in winter rushed down into the Yuba, the gold had settled down and lay thick among the gravel. But most of the parties were sinking, and it was a long way down to the bedrock; for the hills on both sides sloped steeply, and the Yuba must here at one time have rushed through a narrow gorge, until, in some wild freak, it brought down millions of tons of gravel, and resumed its course seventy feet above its former level.

A quarter of a mile higher up a ledge of rock ran across the valley, and over it in the old time the Yuba had poured in a cascade seventy feet deep into the ravine. But the rock now was level with the gravel, only showing its jagged points here and there above it. This ledge had been invaluable to the diggers: without it they could only have sunk their shafts with the greatest difficulty, for the gravel would have been full of water, and even with the greatest pains in puddling and timber work the pumps would scarcely have sufficed to keep it down as it rose in the bottom of the shafts. But the miners had made common cause together, and giving each so many ounces of gold or so many days' work had erected a dam thirty feet high along the ledge of rock, and had cut a channel for the Yuba along the lower slopes of the valley. Of course, when the rain set in, as everybody knew, the dam would go, and the river diggings must be abandoned till the water subsided and a fresh dam was made; but there were two months before them yet, and everyone hoped to be down to the bedrock before the water interrupted their work.

The hillside, both in the Yuba Valley and for some distance along Pine Tree Gulch, was dotted by shanties and tents; the former constructed for the most part of logs roughly squared, the walls being some three feet in height, on which the sharp sloping roof was placed, thatched in the first place with boughs, and made all snug, perhaps, with an old sail stretched over all. The camp was quiet enough during the day. The few women were away with their washing at the pools, a quarter of a mile up the Gulch, and the only persons to be seen about were the men told off for cooking for their respective parties.

But in the evening the camp was lively. Groups of men in red shirts and corded trousers tied at the knee, in high boots, sat round blazing fires, and talked of their prospects or discussed the news of the luck at other camps. The sound of music came from two or three plank erections which rose conspicuously above the huts of the diggers, and were bright externally with the glories of white and colored paints. To and from these men were always sauntering, and it needed not the clink of glasses and the sound of music to tell that they were the bars of the camp.

Here, standing at the counter, or seated at numerous small tables, men were drinking villainous liquor, smoking and talking, and paying but scant attention to the strains of the fiddle or the accordion, save when some well known air was played, when all would join in a boisterous chorus. Some were always passing in or out of a door which led into a room behind. Here there was comparative quiet, for men were gambling, and gambling high.

Going backwards and forwards with liquors into the gambling room of the Imperial Saloon, which stood just where Pine Tree Gulch opened into Yuba Valley, was a lad, whose appearance had earned for him the name of White Faced Dick.

White Faced Dick was not one of those who had done well at Pine Tree Gulch; he had come across the plains with his father, who had died when halfway over, and Dick had been thrown on the world to shift for himself. Nature had not intended him for the work, for he was a delicate, timid lad; what spirits he originally had having been years before beaten out of him by a brutal father. So far, indeed, Dick was the better rather than the worse for the event which had left him an orphan.

They had been traveling with a large party for mutual security against Indians and Mormons, and so long as the journey lasted Dick had got on fairly well. He was always ready to do odd jobs, and as the draught cattle were growing weaker and weaker, and every pound of weight was of importance, no one grudged him his rations in return for his services; but when the company began to descend the slopes of the Sierra Nevada they began to break up, going off by twos and threes to the diggings of which they heard such glowing accounts. Some, however, kept straight on to Sacramento, determining there to obtain news as to the doings at all the different places, and then to choose that which seemed to them to offer the surest prospects of success.

Dick proceeded with them to the town, and there found himself alone. His companions were absorbed in the busy rush of population, and each had so much to provide and arrange for, that none gave a thought to the solitary boy. However, at that time no one who had a pair of hands, however feeble, to work need starve in Sacramento, and for some weeks Dick hung around the town doing odd jobs, and then having saved a few dollars, determined to try his luck at the diggings, and started on foot with a shovel on his shoulders and a few days' provisions slung across it.

Arrived at his destination, the lad soon discovered that gold digging was hard work for brawny and seasoned men, and after a few feeble attempts in spots abandoned as worthless he gave up the effort, and again began to drift; and even in Pine Tree Gulch it was not difficult to get a living. At first he tried rocking cradles, but the work was far harder than it appeared. He was standing ankle deep in water from morning till night, and his cheeks grew paler, and his strength, instead of increasing, seemed to fade away. Still, there were jobs within his strength. He could keep a fire alight and watch a cooking pot, he could carry up buckets of water or wash a flannel shirt, and so he struggled on, until at last some kind hearted man suggested to him that he should try to get a place at the new saloon which was about to be opened.

"You are not fit for this work, young 'un, and you ought to be at home with your mother; if you like I will go up with you this evening to Jeffries. I knew him down on the flats, and I dare say he will take you on. I don't say as a saloon is a good place for a boy, still you will always get your bellyful of victuals and a dry place to sleep in, if it's only under a table. What do you say?"

Dick thankfully accepted the offer, and on Red George's recommendation was that evening engaged. His work was not hard now, for till the miners knocked off there was little doing in the saloon; a few men would come in for a drink at dinnertime, but it was not until the lamps were lit that business began in earnest, and then for four or five hours Dick was busy.

A rougher or healthier lad would not have minded the work, but to Dick it was torture; every nerve in his body thrilled whenever rough miners cursed him for not carrying out their orders more quickly, or for bringing them the wrong liquors, which, as his brain was in a whirl with the noise, the shouting, and the multiplicity of orders, happened frequently. He might have fared worse had not Red George always stood his friend, and Red George was an authority in Pine Tree Gulch—powerful in frame, reckless in bearing and temper, he had been in a score of fights and had come off them, if not unscathed, at least victorious. He was notoriously a lucky digger, but his earnings went as fast as they were made, and he was always ready to open his belt and give a bountiful pinch of dust to any mate down on his luck.

One evening Dick was more helpless and confused than usual. The saloon was full, and he had been shouted at and badgered and cursed until he scarcely knew what he was doing. High play was going on in the saloon, and a good many men were clustered round the table, Red George was having a run of luck, and there was a big pile of gold dust on the table before him. One of the gamblers who was losing had ordered old rye, and instead of bringing it to him, Dick brought a tumbler of hot liquor which someone else had called for. With an oath the man took it up and threw it in his face.

"You cowardly hound!" Red George exclaimed. "Are you man enough to do that to a man?"

"You bet," the gambler, who was a new arrival at Pine Tree Gulch, replied; and picking up an empty glass, he hurled it at Red George. The bystanders sprang aside, and in a moment the two men were facing each other with outstretched pistols. The two reports rung out simultaneously: Red George sat down unconcernedly with a streak of blood flowing down his face, where the bullet had cut a furrow in his cheek; the stranger fell back with a bullet hole in the center of his forehead.

The body was carried outside, and the play continued as if no interruption had taken place. They were accustomed to such occurrences in Pine Tree Gulch, and the piece of ground at the top of the hill, that had been set aside as a burial place, was already dotted thickly with graves, filled in almost every instance by men who had died, in the local phraseology, "with their boots on."

Neither then nor afterwards did Red George allude to the subject to Dick, whose life after this signal instance of his championship was easier than it had hitherto been, for there were few in Pine Tree Gulch who cared to excite Red George's anger; and strangers going to the place were sure to receive a friendly warning that it was best for their health to keep their tempers over any shortcomings on the part of White Faced Dick.

Grateful as he was for Red George's interference on his behalf, Dick felt the circumstance which had ensued more than anyone else in the camp. With others it was the subject of five minutes' talk, but Dick could not get out of his head the thought of the dead man's face as he fell back. He had seen many such frays before, but he was too full of his own troubles for them to make much impression upon him. But in the present case he felt as if he himself was responsible for the death of the gambler; if he had not blundered this would not have happened.

He wondered whether the dead man had a wife and children, and, if so, were they expecting his return? Would they ever hear where he had died, and how?

But this feeling, which, tired out as he was when the time came for closing the bar, often prevented him from sleeping for hours, in no way lessened his gratitude and devotion towards Red George, and he felt that he could die willingly if his life would benefit his champion. Sometimes he thought, too, that his life would not be much to give, for, in spite of shelter and food, the cough which he had caught while working in the water still clung to him, and as his employer said to him angrily one day:

"Your victuals don't do you no good, Dick; you get thinner and thinner, and folks will think as I starve you. Darned if you aint a disgrace to the establishment."

The wind was whistling down the gorges, and the clouds hung among the pine woods which still clothed the upper slopes of the hills, and the diggers, as they turned out one morning, looked up apprehensively.

"But it could not be," they assured each other. Everyone knew that the rains were not due for another month yet; it could only be a passing shower if it rained at all.

But as the morning went on, men came in from camps higher up the river, and reports were current that it had been raining for the last two days among the upper hills; while those who took the trouble to walk across to the new channel could see for themselves at noon that it was filled very nigh to the brim, the water rushing along with thick and turbid current. But those who repeated the rumors, or who reported that the channel was full, were summarily put down. Men would not believe that such a calamity as a flood and the destruction of all their season's work could be impending. There had been some showers, no doubt, as there had often been before, but it was ridiculous to talk of anything like rain a month before its time. Still, in spite of these assertions, there was uneasiness at Pine Tree Gulch, and men looked at the driving clouds above and shook their heads before they went down to the shafts to work after dinner.

When the last customer had left and the bar was closed, Dick had nothing to do till evening, and he wandered outside and sat down on a stump, at first looking at the work going on in the valley, then so absorbed in his own thoughts that he noticed nothing, not even the driving mist which presently set in. He was calculating that he had, with his savings from his wages and what had been given him by the miners, laid by eighty dollars. When he got another hundred and twenty he would go; he would make his way down to San Francisco, and then by ship to Panama and up to New York, and then west again to the village where he was born. There would be people there who would know him, and who would give him work for his mother's sake. He did not care what it was; anything would be better than this. Then his thoughts came back to Pine Tree Gulch, and he started to his feet. Could he be mistaken? Were his eyes deceiving him? No; among the stones and boulders of the old bed of the Yuba there was the gleam of water, and even as he watched it he could see it widening out. He started to run down the hill to give the alarm, but before he was halfway he paused, for there were loud shouts, and a scene of bustle and confusion instantly arose.

The cradles were deserted, and the men working on the surface loaded themselves with their tools and made for the high ground, while those at the windlasses worked their hardest to draw up their comrades below. A man coming down from above stopped close to Dick, with a low cry, and stood gazing with a white scared face. Dick had worked with him; he was one of the company to which Red George belonged.

"What is it, Saunders?"

"My God! they are lost!" the man replied. "I was at the windlass when they shouted up to me to go up and fetch them a bottle of rum. They had just struck it rich, and wanted a drink on the strength of it."

Dick understood at once. Red George and his mates were still in the bottom of the shaft, ignorant of the danger which was threatening them.

"Come on," he cried; "we shall be in time yet," and at the top of his speed dashed down the hill, followed by Saunders.

"What is it, what is it?" asked parties of men mounting the hill.

"Red George's gang are still below."

Dick's eyes were fixed on the water. There was a broad band now of yellow with a white edge down the center of the stony flat, and it was widening with terrible rapidity. It was scarce ten yards from the windlass at the top of Red George's shaft when Dick, followed closely by Saunders, reached it.

"Come up, mates; quick, for your lives! The river is rising; you will be flooded out directly. Everyone else has gone!"

As he spoke he pulled at the rope by which the bucket was hanging, and the handles of the windlass flew round rapidly as it descended. When it had run out Dick and he grasped the handles.

"All right below?"

An answering call came up, and the two began their work, throwing their whole strength into it. Quickly as the windlass revolved it seemed an endless time to Dick before the bucket came up, and the first man stepped out. It was not Red George. Dick had hardly expected it would be. Red George would be sure to see his two mates up before him, and the man uttered a cry of alarm as he saw the water, now within a few feet of the mouth of the shaft.

It was a torrent now, for not only was it coming through the dam, but it was rushing down in cascades from the new channel. Without a word the miner placed himself facing Dick, and the moment the bucket was again down, the three grasped the handles. But quickly as they worked, the edge of the water was within a few inches of the shaft when the next man reached the surface; but again the bucket descended before the rope tightened. However, the water had begun to run over the lip—at first, in a mere trickle, and then, almost instantaneously, in a cascade, which grew larger and larger.

The bucket was halfway up when a sound like thunder was heard, the ground seemed to tremble under their feet, and then at the turn of the valley above, a great wave of yellow water, crested with foam, was seen tearing along at the speed of a race horse.

"The dam has burst!" Saunders shouted. "Run for your lives, or we are all lost!"

The three men dropped the handles and ran at full speed towards the shore, while loud shouts to Dick to follow came from the crowd of men standing on the slope. But the boy grasped the handles, and with lips tightly closed, still toiled on. Slowly the bucket ascended, for Red George was a heavy man; then suddenly the weight slackened, and the handle went round faster. The shaft was filling, the water had reached the bucket, and had risen to Red George's neck, so that his weight was no longer on the rope. So fast did the water pour in, that it was not half a minute before the bucket reached the surface, and Red George sprang out. There was but time for one exclamation, and then the great wave struck them. Red George was whirled like a straw in the current; but he was a strong swimmer, and at a point where the valley widened out, half a mile lower, he struggled to shore.

Two days later the news reached Pine Tree Gulch that a boy's body had been washed ashore twenty miles down, and ten men, headed by Red George, went and brought it solemnly back to Pine Tree Gulch. There among the stumps of pine trees a grave was dug, and there, in the presence of the whole camp, White Faced Dick was laid to rest.

Pine Tree Gulch is a solitude now, the trees are growing again, and none would dream that it was once a busy scene of industry; but if the traveler searches among the pine trees he will find a stone with the words:

"Here lies White Faced Dick, who died to save Red George. 'What can a man do more than give his life for a friend?'"

The text was the suggestion of an ex-clergyman working as a miner in Pine Tree Gulch.

Red George worked no more at the diggings, but, after seeing the stone laid in its place, went east, and with what little money came to him when the common fund of the company was divided after the flood on the Yuba, bought a small farm, and settled down there; but to the end of his life he was never weary of telling those who would listen to it the story of Pine Tree Gulch.

A Brush With The Chinese

It was early in December that H. M. S. Perseus was cruising off the mouth of the Canton River. War had been declared with China in consequence of her continued evasions of the treaty she had made with us, and it was expected that a strong naval force would soon gather to bring her to reason. In the meantime the ships on the station had a busy time of it, chasing the enemy's junks when they ventured to show themselves beyond the reach of the guns of their forts, and occasionally having a brush with the piratical boats which took advantage of the general confusion to plunder friend as well as foe.

The Perseus had that afternoon chased two government junks up a creek. The sun had already set when they took refuge there, and the captain did not care to send his boats after them in the dark, as many of the creeks ran up for miles into the flat country; and as they not unfrequently had many arms or branches, the boats might, in the dark, miss the junk altogether. Orders were issued that four boats should be ready for starting at daybreak the next morning. The Perseus anchored off the mouth of the creek, and two boats were ordered to row backwards and forwards off its mouth all night to insure that the enemy did not slip out in the darkness.

Jack Fothergill, the senior midshipman, was commanding the gig, and two of the other midshipmen were going in the pinnace and launch, commanded respectively by the first lieutenant and the master. The three other midshipmen of the Perseus were loud in their lamentations that they were not to take share in the fun.

"You can't all go, you know," Fothergill said, "and it's no use making a row about it; the captain has been very good to let three of us go."

"It's all very well for you, Jack," Percy Adcock, the youngest of the lads, replied, "because you are one of those chosen; and it is not so hard for Simmons and Linthorpe, because they went the other day in the boat that chased those junks under shelter of the guns of their battery, but I haven't had a chance for ever so long."

"What fun was there in chasing the junks?" Simmons said. "We never got near the brutes till they were close to their battery, and then just as the first shot came singing from their guns, and we thought that we were going to have some excitement, the first lieutenant sung out 'Easy all,' and there was nothing for it but to turn round and to row for the ship, and a nice hot row it was—two hours and a half in a broiling sun. Of course I am not blaming Oliphant, for the captain's orders were strict that we were not to try to cut the junks out if they got under the guns of any of their batteries. Still it was horribly annoying, and I do think the captain might have remembered what beastly luck we had last time, and given us a chance tomorrow."

"It is clear we could not all go," Fothergill said, "and naturally enough the captain chose the three seniors. Besides, if you did have bad luck last time, you had your chance, and I don't suppose we shall have anything more exciting now;

these fellows always set fire to their junks and row for the shore directly they see us, after firing a shot or two wildly in our direction."

"Well, Jack, if you don't expect any fun," Simmons replied, "perhaps you wouldn't mind telling the first lieutenant you do not care for going, and that I am very anxious to take your place. Perhaps he will be good enough to allow me to relieve you."

"A likely thing that!" Fothergill laughed. "No, Tom, I am sorry you are not going, but you must make the best of it till another chance comes."

"Don't you think, Jack," Percy Adcock said to his senior in a coaxing tone later on, "you could manage to smuggle me into the boat with you?"

"Not I, Percy. Suppose you got hurt, what would the captain say then? And firing as wildly as the Chinese do, a shot is just as likely to hit your little carcass as to lodge in one of the sailors. No, you must just make the best of it, Percy, and I promise you that next time there is a boat expedition, if you are not put in, I will say a good word to the first luff for you."

"That promise is better than nothing," the boy said; "but I would a deal rather go this time and take my chance next."

"But you see you can't, Percy, and there's no use talking any more about it. I really do not expect there will be any fighting. Two junks would hardly make any opposition to the boats of the ship, and I expect we shall be back by nine o'clock with the news that they were well on fire before we came up."

Percy Adcock, however, was determined, if possible, to go. He was a favorite among the men, and when he spoke to the bow oar of the gig the latter promised to do anything he could to aid him to carry out his wishes.

"We are to start at daybreak, Tom, so that it will be quite dark when the boats are lowered. I will creep into the gig before that and hide myself as well as I can under your thwart, and all you have got to do is to take no notice of me. When the boat is lowered I think they will hardly make me out from the deck, especially as you will be standing up in the bow holding on with the boat hook till the rest get on board."

"Well, sir, I will do my best; but if you are caught you must not let out that I knew anything about it."

"I won't do that," Percy said. "I don't think there is much chance of my being noticed until we get on board the junks, and then they won't know which boat I came off in, and the first lieutenant will be too busy to blow me up. Of course I shall get it when I am on board again, but I don't mind that so that I see the fun. Besides, I want to send home some things to my sister, and she will like them all the better if I can tell her I captured them on board some junks we seized and burnt."

The next morning the crews mustered before daybreak. Percy had already taken his place under the bow thwart of the gig. The davits were swung overboard, and two men took their places in her as she was lowered down by the falls. As soon as she touched the water the rest of the crew clambered down by the ladder and took their places; then Fothergill took his seat in the stern, and the boat pushed off and lay a few lengths away from the ship until the heavier boats put off. As soon as they were under way Percy crawled out from his hiding place and placed himself in the bow, where he was sheltered by the body of the oarsmen from Fothergill's sight. Day was just breaking now, but it was still dark on the water, and the boat rowed very slowly until it became lighter. Percy could just make out the shores of the creek on both sides; they were but two or three feet above the level of the water, and were evidently submerged at high tide. The creek was about a hundred yards wide, and the lad could not see far ahead, for it was full of sharp windings and turnings. Here and there branches joined it, but the boats were evidently following the main channel. After another half hour's rowing the first lieutenant suddenly gave the order "Easy all," and the men, looking over their shoulders, saw a village a quarter of a mile ahead, with the two junks they had chased the night before lying in front of it. Almost at the same moment a sudden uproar was heard—drums were beaten and gongs sounded.

"They are on the lookout for us," the first lieutenant said. "Mr. Mason, do you keep with me and attack the junk highest up the river; Mr. Bellew and Mr. Fothergill, do you take the one lower down. Row on, men." The oars all touched the water together and the four boats leaped forward. In a minute a scattering fire of gingals and matchlocks was opened from the junks and the bullets pattered on the water round the boats. Percy was kneeling up in the bow now. As they passed a branch channel three or four hundred yards from the village, he started and leaped to his feet.

"There are four or five junks in that passage, Fothergill; they are poling out."

The first lieutenant heard the words.

"Row on, men; let us finish with these craft ahead before the others get out. This must be that piratical village we have heard about, Mr. Mason, as lying up one of these creeks; that accounts for those two junks not going higher up. I was surprised at seeing them here, for they might guess that we should try to get them this morning. Evidently they calculated on catching us in a trap."

Percy was delighted at finding that, in the excitement caused by his news, the first lieutenant had forgotten to take any notice of his being there without orders, and he returned a defiant nod to the threat conveyed by Fothergill shaking his fist at him. As they neared the junks the fire of those on board redoubled, and was aided by that of many villagers gathered on the bank of the creek. Suddenly from a bank of rushes four cannons were fired. A ball struck the pinnace, smashing in her side. The other boats gathered hastily round and took her crew on board, and then dashed at the junks, which were but a hundred yards distant. The valor of the Chinese evaporated as they saw the boats approaching, and scores of them leaped overboard and swam for shore.

In another minute the boats were alongside and the crews scrambling up the sides of the junks. A few Chinamen only attempted to oppose them. These were speedily overcome, and the British had now time to look round, and saw that six junks crowded with men had issued from the side creek and were making towards them.

"Let the boats tow astern," the lieutenant ordered. "We should have to run the gantlet of that battery on shore if we were to attack them, and might lose another boat before we reached their side. We will fight them here."

The junks approached, those on board firing their guns, yelling and shouting, while the drums and gongs were furiously beaten.

"They will find themselves mistaken, Percy, if they think they are going to frighten us with all that row," Fothergill said. "You young rascal, how did you get on board the boat without being seen? The captain will be sure to suspect I had a hand in concealing you."

The tars were now at work firing the gingals attached to the bulwarks and the matchlocks with which the deck was strewn, at the approaching junks. As they took steady aim, leaning their pieces on the bulwarks, they did considerable execution among the Chinamen crowded on board the junks, while the shot of the Chinese, for the most part, whistled far overhead; but the guns of the shore battery, which had now slewed round to bear upon them, opened with a better aim, and several shots came crashing into the sides of the two captured junks.

"Get ready to board, lads!" Lieutenant Oliphant shouted. "Don't wait for them to board you, but the moment they come alongside lash their rigging to ours and spring on board them."

The leading junk was now about twenty yards away, and presently grated alongside. Half a dozen sailors at once sprang into her rigging with ropes, and after lashing the junks together leaped down upon her deck, where Fothergill was leading the gig's crew and some of those rescued from the pinnace, while Mr. Bellew, with another party, had boarded her at the stern. Several of the Chinese fought stoutly, but the greater part lost heart at seeing themselves attacked by the "white devils," instead of, as they expected, overwhelming them by their superior numbers. Many began at once to jump overboard, and after two or three minutes' sharp fighting the rest either followed their example or were beaten below.

Fothergill looked round. The other junk had been attacked by two of the enemy, one on each side, and the little body of sailors were gathered in her waist, and were defending themselves against an overwhelming number of the enemy. The other three piratical junks had been carried somewhat up the creek by the tide that was sweeping inward, and could not for the moment take part in the fight.

"Mr. Oliphant is hard pressed, sir." He asked the master: "Shall we take to the boats?"

"That will be the best plan," Mr. Bellew replied.

"Quick, lads, get the boats alongside and tumble in; there is not a moment to be lost."

The crew at once sprang to the boats and rowed to the other junk, which was but some thirty yards away.

The Chinese, absorbed in their contest with the crew of the pinnace, did not perceive the newcomers until they gained the deck, and with a shout fell furiously upon them. In their surprise and consternation the pirates did not pause to note that they were still five to one superior in number, but made a precipitate rush for their own vessels. The English at once took the offensive. The first lieutenant with his party boarded one, while the newcomers leaped on to the deck of the other. The panic which had seized the Chinese was so complete that they attempted no resistance whatever, but sprang overboard in great numbers and swam to the shore, which was but twenty yards away, and in three minutes the English were in undisputed possession of both vessels.

"Back again, Mr. Fothergill, or you will lose the craft you captured," Lieutenant Oliphant said; "they have already cut her free."

The Chinese, indeed, who had been beaten below by the boarding party, had soon perceived the sudden departure of their captors, and gaining the deck again had cut the lashings which fastened them to the other junk, and were proceeding to hoist their sails. They were too late, however. Almost before the craft had way on her Fothergill and his crew were alongside. The Chinese did not wait for the attack, but at once sprang overboard and made for the shore. The other three junks, seeing the capture of their comrades, had already hoisted their sails and were making up the creek. Fothergill dropped an anchor, left four of his men in charge, and rowed back to Mr. Oliphant.

"What shall we do next, sir?"

"We will give those fellows on shore a lesson, and silence their battery. Two men have been killed since you left. We must let the other junks go for the present. Four of my men were killed and eleven wounded before Mr. Bellew and you came to our assistance. The Chinese were fighting pluckily up to that time, and it would have gone very hard with us if you had not been at hand; the beggars will fight when they think they have got it all their own way. But before we land we will set fire to the five junks we have taken. Do you return and see that the two astern are well lighted, Mr. Fothergill; Mr. Mason will see to these three. When you have done your work take to your boat and lay off till I join you; keep the junks between you and the shore, to protect you from the fire of the rascals."

"I cannot come with you, I suppose, Fothergill?" Percy Adcock said, as the midshipman was about to descend into his boat again.

"Yes, come along, Percy. It doesn't matter what you do now. The captain will be so pleased when he hears that we have captured and burnt five junks, that you will get off with a very light wigging, I imagine."

"That's just what I was thinking, Jack. Has it not been fun?"

"You wouldn't have thought it fun if you had got one of those matchlock balls in your body. There are a good many of our poor fellows just at the present moment who do not see anything funny in the affair at all. Here we are; clamber up."

The crew soon set to work under Fothergill's orders. The sails were cut off the masts and thrown down into the hold; bamboos, of which there were an abundance down there, were heaped over them, a barrel of oil was poured over the mass, and the fire then applied.

"That will do, lads. Now take to your boats and let's make a bonfire of the other junk."

In ten minutes both vessels were a sheet of flame, and the boat was lying a short distance from them waiting for further operations. The inhabitants of the village, furious at the failure of the plan which had been laid for the destruction of the "white devils," kept up a constant fusillade, which, however, did no harm, for the gig was completely sheltered by the burning junks close to her from their missiles.

"There go the others!" Percy exclaimed after a minute or two, as three columns of smoke arose simultaneously from the other junks, and the sailors were seen dropping into their boats alongside.

The killed and wounded were placed in the other gig with four sailors in charge. They were directed to keep under shelter of the junks until rejoined by the pinnace and Fothergill's gig, after these had done their work on shore.

When all was ready the first lieutenant raised his hand as a signal, and the two boats dashed between the burning junks and rowed for the shore. Such of the natives as had their weapons charged fired a hasty volley, and then, as the sailors leapt from their boats, took to their heels.

"Mr. Fothergill, take your party into the village and set fire to the houses; shoot down every man you see. This place is a nest of pirates. I will capture that battery and then join you."

Fothergill and his sailors at once entered the village. The men had already fled; the women were turned out of the houses, and these were immediately set on fire. The tars regarded the whole affair as a glorious joke, and raced from house to house, making a hasty search in each for concealed valuables before setting it on fire. In a short time the whole village was in a blaze.

"There is a house there, standing in that little grove a hundred yards away," Percy said.

"It looks like a temple," Fothergill replied. "However, we will have a look at it." And calling two sailors to accompany him, he started at a run towards it, Percy keeping by his side.

"It is a temple," Fothergill said when they approached it. "Still, we will have a look at it, but we won't burn it; it will be as well to respect the religion, even of a set of piratical scoundrels like these."

At the head of his men he rushed in at the entrance. There was a blaze of fire as half a dozen muskets were discharged in their faces. One of the sailors dropped dead, and before the others had time to realize what had happened they were beaten to the ground by a storm of blows from swords and other weapons.

A heavy blow crashed down on Percy's head, and he fell insensible even before he realized what had occurred.

When he recovered, his first sensation was that of a vague wonder as to what had happened to him. He seemed to be in darkness and unable to move hand or foot. He was compressed in some way that he could not at first understand, and was being bumped and jolted in an extraordinary manner. It was some little time before he could understand the situation. He first remembered the fight with the junks, then he recalled the landing and burning the village; then, as his brain cleared, came the recollection of his start with Fothergill for the temple among the trees, his arrival there, and a loud report and flash of fire.

"I must have been knocked down and stunned," he said to himself, "and I suppose I am a prisoner now to these brutes, and one of them must be carrying me on his back."

Yes, he could understand it all now. His hands and his feet were tied, ropes were passed round his body in every direction, and he was fastened back to back upon the shoulders of a Chinaman. Percy remembered the tales he had heard of the imprisonment and torture of those who fell into the hands of the Chinese, and he bitterly regretted that he had not been killed instead of stunned in the surprise of the temple.

"It would have been just the same feeling," he said to himself, "and there would have been an end of it. Now there is no saying what is going to happen. I wonder whether Jack was killed, and the sailors."

Presently there was a jabber of voices; the motion ceased. Percy could feel that the cords were being unwound, and he was dropped on to his feet; then the cloth was removed from his head, and he could look around.

A dozen Chinese, armed with matchlocks and bristling with swords and daggers, stood around, and among them, bound like himself and gagged by a piece of bamboo forced lengthways across his mouth and kept there with a string going round the back of the head, stood Fothergill. He was bleeding from several cuts in the head. Percy's heart gave a bound of joy at finding that he was not alone; then he tried to feel sorry that Jack had not escaped, but failed to do so, although he told himself that his comrade's presence would not in any way alleviate the fate which was certain to befall him. Still the thought of companionship, even in wretchedness, and perhaps a vague hope that Jack, with his energy and spirit, might contrive some way for their escape, cheered him up.

As Percy, too, was gagged, no word could be exchanged by the midshipmen, but they nodded to each other. They were now put side by side and made to walk in the center of their captors. On the way they passed through several villages, whose inhabitants poured out to gaze at the captives, but the men in charge of them were evidently not disposed to delay, as they passed through without a stop. At last they halted before two cottages standing by themselves, thrust the prisoners into a small room, removed their gags, and left them entirely to themselves.

"Well, Percy, my boy, so they caught you too? I am awfully sorry. It was my fault for going with only two men into that temple, but as the village had been deserted and scarcely a man was found there, it never entered my mind that there might be a party in the temple."

"Of course not, Jack; it was a surprise altogether. I don't know anything about it, for I was knocked down, I suppose, just as we went in, and the first thing I knew about it was that I was being carried on the back of one of those fellows. I thought it was awful at first, but I don't seem to mind so much now you are with me."

"It is a comfort to have someone to speak to," Jack said, "yet I wish you were not here, Percy; I can't do you any good, and I shall never cease blaming myself for having brought you into this scrape. I don't know much more about the affair than you do. The guns were fired so close to us that my face was scorched with one of them, and almost at the same instant I got a lick across my cheek with a sword. I had just time to hit at one of them, and then almost at the same moment I got two or three other blows, and down I went; they threw themselves on the top of me and tied and gagged me in no time. Then I was tied to a long bamboo, and two fellows put the ends on their shoulders and went off with me through the fields. Of course I was face downwards, and did not know you were with us till they stopped and loosed me from the bamboo and set me on my feet."

"But what are they going to do with us, do you think, Jack?"

"I should say they are going to take us to Canton and claim a reward for our capture, and there I suppose they will cut off our heads or saw us in two, or put us to some other unpleasant kind of death. I expect they are discussing it now; do you hear what a jabber they are kicking up?"

Voices were indeed heard raised in angry altercation in the next room. After a time the din subsided and the conversation appeared to take a more amiable turn.

"I suppose they have settled it as far as they are concerned," Jack said; "anyhow, you may be quite sure they mean to make something out of us. If they hadn't they would have finished us at once, for they must have been furious at the destruction of their junks and village. As to the idea that mercy has anything to do with it, we may as well put it out of our minds. The Chinaman, at the best of times, has no feeling of pity in his nature, and after their defeat it is certain they would have killed us at once had they not hoped to do better by us. If they had been Indians I should have said they had carried us off to enjoy the satisfaction of torturing us, but I don't suppose it is that with them."

"Do you think there is any chance of our getting away?" Percy asked, after a pause.

"I should say not the least in the world, Percy. My hands are fastened so tight now that the ropes seem cutting into my wrists, and after they had set me on my feet and cut the cords of my legs I could scarcely stand at first, my feet were so numbed by the pressure. However, we must keep up our pluck. Possibly they may keep us at Canton for a bit, and if they do the squadron may arrive and fight its way past the forts and take the city before they have quite made up their minds as to what kind of death will be most appropriate to the occasion. I wonder what they are doing now? They seem to be chopping sticks."

"I wish they would give us some water," Percy said. "I am frightfully thirsty."

"And so am I, Percy; there is one comfort, they won't let us die of thirst, they could get no satisfaction out of our deaths now."

Two hours later some of the Chinese re-entered the room and led the captives outside, and the lads then saw what was the meaning of the noise they had heard. A cage had been manufactured of strong bamboos. It was about four and a half feet long, four feet wide, and less than three feet high; above it was fastened two long bamboos. Two or three of the bars of the cage had been left open.

"My goodness! they never intend to put us in there," Percy exclaimed.

"That they do," Jack said. "They are going to carry us the rest of the way."

The cords which bound the prisoners' hands were now cut, and they were motioned to crawl into the cage. This they did; the bars were then put in their places and securely lashed. Four men went to the ends of the poles and lifted the cage upon their shoulders; two others took their places beside it, and one man, apparently the leader of the party, walked on ahead; the rest remained behind.

"I never quite realized what a fowl felt in a coop before," Jack said, "but if its sensations are at all like mine they must be decidedly unpleasant. It isn't high enough to sit upright in, it is nothing like long enough to lie down, and as to getting out one might as well think of flying. Do you know, Percy, I don't think they mean taking us to Canton at all. I did not think of it before, but from the direction of the sun I feel sure that we cannot have been going that way. What they are up to I can't imagine."

In an hour they came to a large village. Here the cage was set down and the villagers closed round. They were, however, kept a short distance from the cage by the men in charge of it. Then a wooden platter was placed on the ground, and persons throwing a few copper coins into this were allowed to come near the cage.

"They are making a show of us!" Fothergill exclaimed. "That's what they are up to, you see if it isn't; they are going to travel up country to show the 'white devils' whom their valor has captured."

This was, indeed, the purpose of the pirates. At that time Europeans seldom ventured beyond the limits assigned to them in the two or three towns where they were permitted to trade, and few, indeed, of the country people had ever obtained a sight of the white barbarians of whose doings they had so frequently heard. Consequently a small crowd soon gathered round the cage, eyeing the captives with the same interest they would have felt as to unknown and dangerous beasts; they laughed and joked, passed remarks upon them, and even poked them with sticks. Fothergill, furious at this treatment, caught one of the sticks, and wrenching it from the hands of the Chinaman tried to strike at him through the bars, a proceeding which excited shouts of laughter from the bystanders.

"I think, Jack," Percy said, "it will be best to try and keep our tempers and not to seem to mind what they do to us, then if they find they can't get any fun out of us they will soon leave us alone."

"Of course, that's the best plan," Fothergill agreed, "but it's not so easy to follow. That fellow very nearly poked out my eye with his stick, and no one's going to stand that if he can help it."

It was some hours before the curiosity of the village was satisfied. When all had paid who were likely to do so, the guards broke up their circle, and leaving two of their number at the cage to see that no actual harm was caused to their prisoners, the rest went off to a refreshment house. The place of the elders was now taken by the boys and children of the village, who crowded round the cage, prodded the prisoners with sticks, and, putting their hands through the bars, pulled their ears and hair. This amusement, however, was brought to an abrupt conclusion by Fothergill suddenly seizing the wrist of a big boy and pulling his arm through the cage until his face was against the bars; then he proceeded to punch him until the guard, coming to his rescue, poked Fothergill with his stick until he released his hold.

The punishment of their comrade excited neither anger nor resentment among the other boys, who yelled with delight at his discomfiture, but it made them more careful in approaching the cage, and though they continued to poke the prisoners with sticks they did not venture again to thrust a hand through the bars. At sunset the guards again came round, lifted the cage and carried it into a shed. A platter of dirty rice and a jug of water were put into the cage; two of the men lighted their long pipes and sat down on guard beside it, and, the doors being closed, the captives were left in peace.

"If this sort of thing is to go on, as I suppose it is," Fothergill said, "the sooner they cut off our heads the better."

"It is very bad, Jack. I am sore all over with those probes from their sharp sticks."

"I don't care for the pain, Percy, so much as the humiliation of the thing. To be stared at and poked at as if we were wild beasts by these curs, when with half a dozen of our men we could send a hundred of them scampering, I feel as if I could choke with rage."

"You had better try and eat some of this rice, Jack. It is beastly, but I dare say we shall get no more until tomorrow night, and we must keep up our strength if we can. At any rate, the water is not bad, that's a comfort."

"No thanks to them," Jack growled. "If there had been any bad water in the neighborhood they would have given it to us."

For two weeks the sufferings of the prisoners continued. Their captors avoided towns where the authorities would probably at once have taken the prisoners out of their hands. No one would have recognized the two captives as the midshipmen of the Perseus; their clothes were in rags—torn to pieces by the thrusts of the sharp pointed bamboos, to which they had daily been subjected—the bad food, the cramped position, and the misery which they suffered had worn both lads to skeletons; their hair was matted with filth, their faces begrimed with dirt. Percy was so weak that he felt he could not stand. Fothergill, being three years older, was less exhausted, but he knew that he, too, could not support his sufferings for many days longer. Their bodies were covered with sores, and try as they would they were able to catch only a few minutes' sleep at a time so much did the bamboo bars hurt their wasted limbs.

They seldom exchanged a word during the daytime, suffering in silence the persecutions to which they were exposed, but at night they talked over their homes and friends in England, and their comrades on board ship, seldom saying a word as to their present position. They were now in a hilly country, but had not the least idea of the direction in which it lay from Canton or its distance from the coast.

One evening Jack said to his companion, "I think it's nearly all over now, Percy. The last two days we have made longer journeys, and have not stopped at any of the smaller villages we passed through. I fancy our guards must see that we can't last much longer, and are taking us down to some town to hand us over to the authorities and get their reward for us."

"I hope it is so, Jack; the sooner the better. Not that it makes much difference now to me, for I do not think I can stand many more days of it."

"I am afraid I am tougher than you, Percy, and shall take longer to kill, so I hope with all my heart that I may be right, and that they may be going to give us up to the authorities."

The next evening they stopped at a large place, and were subjected to the usual persecution; this, however, was now less prolonged than during the early days of their captivity, for they had now no longer strength or spirits to resent their treatment, and as no fun was to be obtained from passive victims, even the village boys soon ceased to find any amusement in tormenting them.

When most of their visitors had left them, an elderly Chinaman approached the side of the cage. He spoke to their guard and looked at them attentively for some minutes, then he said in pigeon English, "You officer men?"

"Yes!" Jack exclaimed, starting at the sound of the English words, the first they had heard spoken since their captivity. "Yes, we are officers of the Perseus."

"Me speeke English velly well," the Chinaman said; "me pilot man many years on Canton River. How you get here?"

"We were attacking some piratical junks, and landed to destroy the village where the people were firing on us. We entered a place full of pirates, and were knocked down and taken prisoners and carried away up the country; that is six weeks ago, and you see what we are now."

"Pirate men velly bad," the Chinaman said; "plunder many junk on river and kill crew. Me muchee hate them."

"Can you do anything for us?" Jack asked. "You will be well rewarded if you could manage to get us free."

The man shook his head.

"Me no see what can do, me stranger here; come to stay with wifey; people no do what me ask them. English ships attack Canton, much fight and take town, people all hate English. Bad country dis. People in one village fight against another. Velly bad men here."

"How far is Canton away?" Jack asked. "Could you not send down to tell the English we are here?"

"Fourteen days' journey off," the man said; "no see how can do anything."

"Well," Jack said, "when you get back again to Canton let our people know what has been the end of us; we shall not last much longer."

"All light," the man said; "will see what me can do. Muchee think tonight!"

And after saying a few words to the guards, who had been regarding this conversation with an air of surprise, the Chinaman retired.

The guards had for some time abandoned the precaution of sitting up at night by the cage, convinced that their captives had no longer strength to attempt to break through its fastenings or to drag themselves many yards away if they could do so. They therefore left it standing in the open, and, wrapping themselves in their thickly wadded coats, for the nights were cold, lay down by the side of the cage.

The coolness of the nights had, indeed, assisted to keep the two prisoners alive. During the day the sun was excessively hot, and the crowd of visitors round the cage impeded the circulation of the air and added to their sufferings. It was true that the cold at night frequently prevented them from sleeping, but it acted as a tonic and braced them up.

"What did he mean about the villages attacking each other?" Percy asked.

"I have heard," Jack replied, "that in some parts of China things are very much the same as they used to be in the highlands of Scotland. There is no law or order. The different villages are like clans, and wage war on each other. Sometimes the government sends a number of troops, who put the thing down for a time, chop off a good many heads, and then march away, and the whole work begins again as soon as their backs are turned."

That night the uneasy slumber of the lads was disturbed by a sudden firing; shouts and yells were heard, and the firing redoubled. "The village is attacked," Jack said. "I noticed that, like some other places we have come into lately, there is a strong earthen wall round it, with gates. Well, there is one comfort—it does not make much difference to us which side wins."

The guards at the first alarm leaped to their feet, caught up their matchlocks, and ran to aid in the defense of the wall. Two minutes later a man ran up to the cage.

"All lightee," he said; "just what me hopee."

With his knife he cut the tough withes that held the bamboos in their places, and pulled out three of the bars.

"Come along," he said; "no time to lose."

Jack scrambled out, but in trying to stand upright gave a sharp exclamation of pain. Percy crawled out more slowly; he tried to stand up, but could not. The Chinaman caught him up and threw him on his shoulder.

"Come along quickee," he said to Jack; "if takee village, kill evely one." He set off at a run. Jack followed as fast as he could, groaning at every step from the pain the movement caused to his bruised body.

They went to the side of the village opposite to that at which the attack was going on. They met no one on the way, the inhabitants having all rushed to the other side to repel the attack. They stopped at a small gate in the wall, the Chinaman drew back the bolts and opened it, and they passed out into the country. For an hour they kept on. By the end of that time Jack could scarcely drag his limbs along. The Chinaman halted at length in a clump of trees surrounded by a thick undergrowth.

"Allee safe here," he said, "no searchee so far; here food," and he produced from a wallet a cold chicken and some boiled rice, and unslung from his shoulder a gourd filled with cold tea.

"Me go back now, see what happen. Tomollow nightee come again— bringee more food." And without another word went off at a rapid pace.

Jack moistened his lips with the tea, and then turned to his companion. Percy had not spoken a word since he had been released from the cage, and had been insensible during the greater part of his journey. Jack poured some cold tea between his lips.

"Cheer up, Percy, old boy, we are free now, and with luck and that good fellow's help we will work our way down to Canton yet."

"I shall never get down there; you may," Percy said feebly.

"Oh, nonsense, you will pick up strength like a steam engine now. Here, let me prop you against this tree. That's better. Now drink a drop of this tea; it's like nectar after that filthy water we have been drinking. Now you will feel better. Now you must try and eat a little of this chicken and rice. Oh, nonsense, you have got to do it. I am not going to let you give way when our trouble is just over. Think of your people at home, Percy, and make an effort for their sakes.

Good Heavens! now I think of it, it must be Christmas morning. We were caught on the 2d and we have been just twenty-two days on show. I am sure that it must be past twelve o'clock, and it is Christmas Day. It is a good omen, Percy. This food isn't like roast beef and plum pudding, but it's not to be despised. I can tell you. Come, fire away, that's a good fellow."

Percy made an effort and ate a few mouthfuls of rice and chicken, then he took another draught of tea, and lay down, and was almost immediately asleep.

Jack ate his food slowly and contentedly till he finished half the supply, then he, too, lay down, and after a short but hearty thanksgiving for his escape from a slow and lingering death, he too, fell off to sleep. The sun was rising when he woke, being aroused by a slight movement on the part of Percy; he opened his eyes and sat up.

"Well, Percy, how do you feel this morning?" he asked cheerily.

"I feel too weak to move," Percy replied languidly.

"Oh, you will be all right when you have sat up and eaten breakfast," Jack said. "Here you are; here is a wing for you, and this rice is as white as snow, and the tea is first rate. I thought last night after I lay down that I heard a murmur of water, so after we have had breakfast I will look about and see if I can find it. We should feel like new men after a wash. You look awful, and I am sure I am just as bad."

The thought of a wash inspirited Percy far more than that of eating, and he sat up and made a great effort to do justice to breakfast. He succeeded much better than he had done the night before, and Jack, although he pretended to grumble, was satisfied with his companion's progress, and finished off the rest of the food. Then he set out to search for water. He had not very far to go; a tiny stream, two feet wide and several inches deep, ran through the wood from the higher ground. After throwing himself down and taking a drink, he hurried back to Percy.

"It is all right, Percy, I have found it. We can wash to our hearts' content; think of that, lad."

Percy could hardly stand, but he made an effort, and Jack half carried him to the streamlet. There the lads spent two hours. First they bathed their heads and hands, and then, stripping, lay down in the stream and allowed it to flow over them, then they rubbed themselves with handfuls of leaves dipped in the water, and when they at last put on their rags again felt like new men. Percy was able to walk back to the spot they had quitted with the assistance only of Jack's arm. The latter, feeling that his breakfast had by no means appeased his hunger, now started for a search through the wood, and presently returned to Percy laden with nuts and berries.

"The nuts are sure to be all right; I expect the berries are too. I have certainly seen some like them in native markets, and I think it will be quite safe to risk it."

The rest of the day was spent in picking nuts and eating them. Then they sat down and waited for the arrival of their friend. He came two hours after nightfall with a wallet stored with provisions, and told them that he had regained the village unobserved. The attack had been repulsed, but with severe loss to the defenders as well as the assailants; two of their guards had been among the killed. The others had made a great clamor over the escape of the prisoners, and had made a close search throughout the village and immediately round it, for they were convinced that their captives had not had the strength to go any distance. He thought, however, that although they had professed the greatest indignation, and had offered many threats as to the vengeance that government would take upon the village, one of whose inhabitants, at least, must have aided in the evasion of the prisoners, they would not trouble themselves any further in the matter. They had already reaped a rich harvest from the exhibition, and would divide among themselves the share of their late comrades; nor was it at all improbable that if they were to report the matter to the authorities they would themselves get into serious trouble for not having handed over the prisoners immediately after their capture.

For a fortnight the pilot nursed and fed the two midshipmen. He had already provided them with native clothes, so that if by chance any villagers should catch sight of them they would not recognize them as the escaped white men. At the end of that time both the lads had almost recovered from the effects of their sufferings. Jack, indeed, had picked up from the first, but Percy for some days continued so weak and ill that Jack had feared that he was going to have an attack of fever of some kind. His companion's cheery and hopeful chat did as much good for Percy as the nourishing food with which their friend supplied them, and at the end of the fortnight he declared that he felt sufficiently strong to attempt to make his way down to the coast.

The pilot acted as their guide. When they inquired about his wife, he told them carelessly that she would remain with her kinsfolk, and would travel on to Canton and join him there when she found an opportunity. The journey was accomplished at night, by very short stages at first, but by increasing distances as Percy gained strength. During the daytime the lads lay hid in woods or jungles, while their companion went into the village and purchased food. They struck the river many miles above Canton, and the pilot, going down first to a village on its banks, bargained for a boat to take him and two women down to the city.

The lads went on board at night and took their places in the little cabin formed of bamboos and covered with mats in the stern of the boat, and remained thus sheltered not only from the view of people in boats passing up or down the stream, but from the eyes of their own boatmen.

After two days' journey down the river without incident, they arrived off Canton, where the British fleet was still lying while negotiations for peace were being carried on with the authorities at Pekin. Peeping out between the mats, the lads caught sight of the English warships, and, knowing that there was now no danger, they dashed out of the cabin, to the surprise of the native boatmen, and shouted and waved their arms to the distant ships.

In ten minutes they were alongside the Perseus, when they were hailed as if restored from the dead. The pilot was very handsomely rewarded by the English authorities for his kindness to the prisoners, and was highly satisfied with the result of his proceedings, which more than doubled the little capital with which he had retired from business. Jack Fothergill and Percy Adcock declare that they have never since eaten chicken without thinking of their

Christmas fare on the morning of their escape from the hands of the Chinese pirates.

THE END.

G. A. Henty

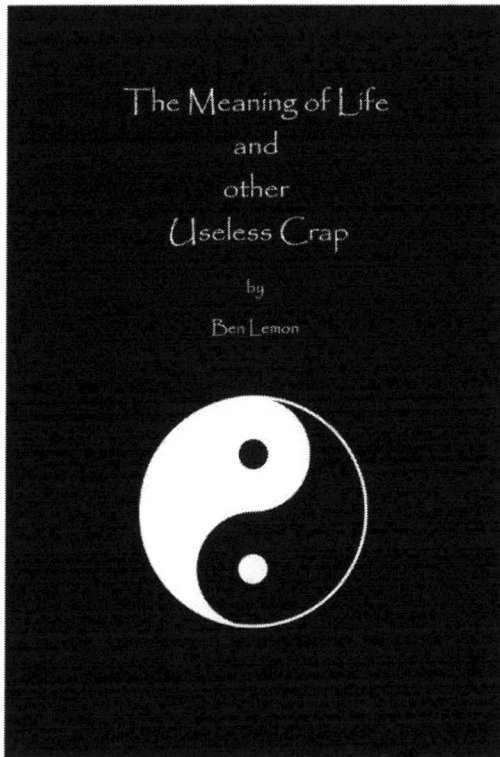

The Meaning of Life and Other Useless Crap is perhaps our generations greatest work as it answers the age old question "What is the meaning of life?" Written simply and straightforward it is easy to understand why Ben Lemon is the most important living philosopher. It hasn't been since A Modest Proposal that a pamphlet can our perceptions so dramatically.

Made in the USA
Las Vegas, NV
10 August 2021